Never Stop Dreaming……

Brian Jay Nelson

Branchview – The Unexpected Journey

–By Brian Jay Nelson

Table of Contents

Chapter One:

Lockeport Harbor, Connecticut Autumn 2018

As the sun nestled deep in the horizon, the crisp biting chill of evening fell upon the sleeping town. Opening the door for the stars to make their presence known, twinkling across the night sky. An awkward presence crept quietly through the woods behind a quaint cottage along the walking path. Peter McAndrew, a stocky man in his early fifties, snuck across the backyard toward a lighted window.

In the cover of darkness, he went unnoticed despite a window being open slightly, casting a dim light across the back yard. He was drawn to the pleasurable moans coming from inside the room. Intent on snooping, he grabbed a few split logs from the nearby woodpile and used them to step up to see the scene inside. Peter watched with a perverted grin as he spied a couple making love.

The sight was entrancing and held him hostage for a few long moments until, without warning, something unfathomable happened. As the fear of the moment rushed over his body, he became frozen, unable to move. *Oh my, this can't be…* he thought to himself. As the overwhelming distress averted his consciousness, a peering set of eyeballs from a grotesque beast turned in his direction from inside the dimly lit room. The intense situation took control once more, leaving Peter apprehensive as to his next move. The loosely placed wood collapsed under his feet, sending him crashing to the ground with a loud thud.

A gnashing growl emerged from the inside of the room as he lay on the ground looking up at the window, trembling in fear. His mind demanded he get up and run, yet somehow, he remained immobile. Finally, after the battle in his head calmed for a split-second, he got up to run, but fear slowed his process

He turns to see the Branchview pathway, clearly glistening in the moonlight. His only intention was aimed at finding safety in the main house, and he took off in a dead run. However, in his physical condition, the best he could muster was a jog. As he approached the fountain, he figured it to be halfway to the house, and fear rushed over his frame once again, as he turned to look behind him. Out of breath and panting, he almost tripped over his own two feet. The path behind Peter was empty, but he could feel the hairs on the back of his neck stand up, as he heard wisps of wind rushing through the air around him.

It seemed as though the path lengthened the more, he ran toward his goal. He envisioned the large oak doors with the lion's head knocker, and a kind member of the Branch family urgently ushering him to safety inside the great house. It was his only chance to escape.

As he approached the giant wooden doors, he was almost crawling. *Oh, my if I survive this I have to get into better shape,* he thought to himself. Panicked, he grabbed the knocker, yelling frantically "Help! Someone, please help!" Peter continued to beat the knocker passionately against the wooden door, screaming "Help! Please let me in---"

A hideous apparition rushed past the evergreens lining the front of the old house, and he could feel a cold breeze brush his face. The pounding of the knocker rivaled the intense pounding of his heart. Suddenly a loud creaking noise emerged above him, and he looked upward, only to see it was far too late to react. His final thoughts finished with a terrifying scream, as a large part of the building façade that had broken loose, crashed down on top of him.

In the Gothic-styled writing room, author Steven Spencer, an athletically built man in his mid-thirties, with a sober face, and handsomely chiseled features, sat behind his antique desk, focused on his Apple computer.

The marble tiled flooring and cherry woodwork in the room created an alluring atmosphere that worked to enhance his creative genius. He glanced up to admire his library of books that filled an entire wall. He grabbed hold of his cup of coffee as he got up and paced slowly toward the large picture window overlooking a green, beautifully manicured lawn. On the way, he paused to run his fingers over the smooth surface of The Angel of Sorrow Statue that sat prominently on a pedestal in the center of the room. He closed his eyes to savor the moment, hoping that the touch might relieve his stubborn writer's block.

In his mind, he began rehearsing the words that came. "In the early days of November when shadows fall early and the days end in the late afternoon, it's said that spirits become more active. They feed off the energy of the long nights. It's as though Halloween ushered in the season of darkness, death, and a biting cold that is felt most commonly in the northern hemisphere." He smiled as his words sounded appealing.

While he wandered the office, he cradled his cup of coffee in his hands, as if drawing inspiration from the liquid gold within. *Yes,* he thought, as he settled himself behind the desk once more.

His thoughts continued to race as he leaned back in his plush leather chair. "On this pleasant South Florida evening, I feel uncomfortably and strangely drawn to a small town on the northern Atlantic coast that I only know from my recent dreams."

His fingers began to tap away at the keyboard as the words continued to flow. "A gentle rain mists my shoulders and I can almost feel the damp chill of the ocean. The dark gray skies work to achieve the perfect atmosphere, and the air is filled with the smell of limp, wet, decaying leaves that I trample underfoot as I walk in this unfamiliar place." Steven lost all conscious thought, and before he could type any further, the words seemed to appear on the screen magically. The scene took him completely by surprise, and his chair gently pulled him backward, as he stared at the screen in confusion.

A few seconds later, a large bold print appeared on the monitor: "You must go to Branchview." Steven cocked his head, struggling to determine the meaning behind the message. He gently raised his arms, folding his fingers behind his head with a sigh, as two cold hands gripped his shoulders from behind.

"Steven… is everything alright?" He nearly jumped out of his skin with the unexpected entrance of his domestic partner.

Fellow author Loraine Sandstrom, an incredibly attractive, willowy brunette with a proper British accent, affectionately draped her arms around him. "Did I scare you, Mr. Spencer?" she snickered.

"I certainly didn't expect anyone to sneak up behind me."

Still amused, "I'm so sorry, but it was impossible to resist." Loraine had a way of moving through the house in complete silence.

Steven turned to address her, "Your hands are as cold as death."

"I just took some food from the freezer… and you know I have naturally cold hands."

Steven looked at her with an intensely serious expression, "The strangest thing just happened before you walked in.

"Really? Please do tell me about it."

Steven gestured toward his computer, "Look—"

Loraine, "Look at what…?"

He appeared dumbfounded, "What?! I don't understand, they were here in all caps. Words I did not type, or would even say. They just appeared out of nowhere." Loraine stayed calm to appease his frame of mind.

"Obviously, now they're gone. What did they say?"

"It told me to go to Branchview."

"Where on earth is Branchview?"

"I was hoping maybe you'd know." Steven sighed.

"Well, perhaps it's time to take a break. You have been at this since the early morning. Go out and get some fresh air. Clear your head."

Loraine grabbed the dog leash from the basket next to his desk. "Bumpers needs a walk." Their Boston Terrier crossed the room in several leaps; his large brown eyes pleaded for some attention. "Would you take him out for a while, dear? I desperately need to call our agent to find out what dates he set up for our book signings."

"Fine…" he scoffed. She smirked when Steven took the leash. Bumpers let out an intense whine of relief. Loraine smiled and left dog and master to their daily routine.

Steven opened the patio door and waited for Bumpers to follow close behind. A cool evening breeze caressed his face, it felt good to get some fresh air. *Loraine was right, I needed a break. I must have been getting tired.* It was easy to talk with Bumpers on their walk, he was a great listener.

It took them the better part of an hour to walk the outer edge of the lawn before sunset. The stroll calmed his apprehensions, but he could not shake the image of what had happened. Steven struggled to make sense of the message. Did he write the words or was something else amiss? He practiced freewriting regularly to hone his writing skills; nonetheless, he had never typed a sentence without his knowledge.

After supper, Steven went upstairs with Bumpers, while Loraine worked on her latest novel in her study. He turned on the TV, trying to take his mind off the earlier experience. However, it was to no avail. It was going to take more than a show to alter his thoughts.

By the time Loraine came upstairs several hours later, Steven and Bumpers were fast asleep on the bed. The sight brought a smile to her face, it tickled her soul to see the content. She moved Bumpers over between them and crawled into bed. It did not take long before Loraine was fast asleep; one thing she never suffered from was insomnia.

A few hours into the night, Steven became restless in his sleep. He mumbled, thrashing from side to side. Then, a sudden chill moved through the room and immediately brought him to attention. In the darkened room, Steven saw a pair of eyes, a menacing glare directly on him. The bedroom door creaked open, changing the light in the room, and he paused, waiting for the horrifying experience to worsen. Suddenly, Steven half-awoke from his deep dream to a wet, sloppy tongue licking his face.

The commotion woke Loraine. "Oh, Steven! You shouldn't let Bumpers lick you on the mouth."

"Bumpers, oh you… go away," he mumbled, as he sat up in bed and wiped his mouth unpleasantly.

"Steven-" Loraine began.

"I thought that was your tongue."

"Oh, really, Steven! Do you expect me to believe you were dreaming of us having sex?"

"You're right…" He smiled. "Actually, I dreamt that I was walking down a path with a strange woman. I didn't see her face, and there was a lot of fog."

"So! There is another woman?"

Steven shrugged off her comment and continued. "Anyway! We walked up to this old Victorian mansion with a large wood door, and lions head knocker."

Loraine responded with disdain, "And then, you no doubt entered, and started having wild, unbridled sex with this woman?"

"No! I woke up thinking it was your tongue circling my mouth." Steven smirked. "It's highly unbelievable that you thought it was my tongue." Loraine sat up; her feelings hurt.

"Forget it, I give up!" He glanced over at the clock and got out of bed. "It's three o'clock in the morning, and since I'm awake anyway, maybe I can get some work done." Loraine acknowledged with an indignant grunt.

The last thing Steven wanted was to be up that early, but the dream along with what happened that afternoon had stirred up some feelings that nagged at him. Plus, although he loved Loraine, sometimes she could get on his nerves.

"I'm going downstairs, go back to sleep." He grabbed his slippers and hopped down the hallway. In actuality, Steven loved the early mornings before the world woke to disturb the peace, however, that was a pleasure he kept to himself.

As he approached the desk in his study, Steven paused and stared at the screen of his computer. Would he receive another note? *Well, here we go…* he muttered. On the corner of the desk was an antique Tiffany lamp that he picked up at an auction several years ago. It gave off the perfect, warm glow in the early morning without being stark. He switched on the computer and sat down.

The lights on the monitor suddenly flickered. Steven grew nervous as a cold chill swept through the room. He looked up to verify the ceiling fan had not been turned on. He could feel a presence in the room, but no one else was there. *What is going on here?* A few seconds later his attention was averted to Bumpers entering the room. As Steven looked back toward the screen, letters began to appear. He waited for it to finish. "Lockeport, Connecticut."

Steven sat back in his chair with a sigh, trying to figure out the great mystery. However, he learned after the last time to make notes of the wording. Only, now his interest was piqued, so he forgot about his novel and did some research. The first order of business, Lockeport Connecticut. His Google search found some interesting aspects worth further studying. Before long, the hours had passed and he heard their housekeeper, Mrs. Porter, rustling around in the kitchen.

In quest of an essential cup of coffee, Steven got up and sauntered into the kitchen.

As he entered the room, Mrs. Porter turned to look up at Steven. She stood five foot two with poor posture. "Coffee, Mr. Spencer?"

"That would be heavenly, Mrs. Porter."

Loraine strolled into the kitchen a few minutes later. "I'll have one as well, Mrs. Porter." She sat down across from Steven, still perturbed from the incident earlier that morning. "Darling! Did you have any more wet dreams last night?"

"Do we have to continue with that?" he sighed indignantly.

Mrs. Porter rolled her eyes as she poured Loraine some coffee. "I suppose not—"

Steven took a sigh of relief and lowered the paper. "It happened again."

"What happened, may I ask?"

Steven looked indignant. "The words on my screen… did you forget already?"

"Oh, that. And?"

"I think I'm supposed to go to Lockeport, Connecticut."

"Really… because your computer went crazy and typed some words on the screen? Or is that where that little trollop from your dream lives?"

Mrs. Porter glanced over her shoulder with a raised brow as she busied herself cleaning the kitchen counter, "Loraine…" His voice lowered. "Enough with the woman in my dream. Something or someone is trying to communicate with me."

"Fine… If you truly believe that's the case, what do you plan to do about it?"

Steven answered with a shrug, "I guess follow up on it. Besides, I could use a vacation. Who knows, it might turn into a great novel."

Loraine cast a serious look of warning across the table, "Just be careful with your curiosity. This appears to be somewhat paranormal, and you and I both have a tad bit of familiarity with that subject."

Mrs. Porter's persona changed in an instant. She cast a long nervous glance over her shoulder as Loraine exited the room. Steven sat in silence contemplating the situation. He looked up when Mrs. Porter walked over and laid a weathered bony hand on his shoulder. "Please be safe, Mr. Spencer. Something feels strange about all this."

"I'll be just fine. It's just a way to appease my curiosity; solve this mystery. I'll be back here in no time."

She walked away in a huff. "Just remember what they say about curiosity killing the cat." Steven knew all too well what the warning meant.

Chapter Two:

The Adventure Begins

Steven smoothed things over with Loraine before he left on his adventure. However, Mrs. Porter was another story; she had been his nanny while growing up. She never married, and Steven took her on as his housekeeper after his parents died, and she had nowhere else to go. He was the only family she had. Either way, it was a calling he had to see through to the end.

Steven caught an early morning flight to Boston, then leased a car for the hour-long drive to the Connecticut coast. He arrived in the quaint town of Lockeport just before noon. The growling in his stomach reminded him that he had not yet eaten breakfast. As he drove down the main street, desperately looking for a restaurant, he spotted a 1950's style place called The City Diner. He'd always liked the old fashioned, mom and pop breakfast joints, and was pleased to find one in this little town.

An entrance bell rang, alerting the customers when Steven entered the restaurant. It seemed to be the local hangout; a perfect place to learn all the gossip. One of the bar stools at the counter was open, so Steven snatched it up. A cute waitress met him with a smile.

"Good morning, what can I get you to drink?"

Steven looked at her name tag, "Hello—Suzie?" She smiled. "I'll take a cup of coffee to start."

"Coming right up," she stated with pizzazz.

Steven watched her brunette curls bounce as she moved down the counter to grab a cup and the coffee pot. Suzie was a young girl in her late teens, freshly out of high school. A personable, light-hearted individual, ready to take on the world. It made Steven think briefly of his youth; a young dedicated writer striving to make it to the big times as a best-selling author.

Suzie returned with a steaming hot cup of coffee. Then, she handed him a menu. "Are you new in town?"

"No, just visiting. You have a nice little town here."

Suzy replied jokingly, "It's a nice place, but it's not too exciting."

"Oh, I'm sure a town like this has some unique and mysterious attributes." He smiled. Steven knew just how to get attention from the ladies, when necessary. "Have you by chance ever heard of a place around here called Branchview?"

"Yes. I have a good friend that lives there."

A grizzled voice cracked from the stool beside Steven, with a strong New England brogue. "You don't want to go there, mister." The old man pointed a warning finger at Steven, "Nothing good ever happens at that place." The statement caught Steven's attention.

"Really?"

"Darn tooting! Just this past week, one of the groundskeepers was crushed when a large part of the facade broke loose. He never knew what hit him."

'That's terrible!"

"I'll tell you right now that no one in town, including myself, thinks it was an accident."

Lucretia (Lucia) Darknight, a striking blonde bombshell in her late twenties, wearing a shapely red dress with lipstick and fingernails to match, sauntered up from behind.

"Now just hold on… It's not polite to scare our visitors. We have a fine upstanding community." The statement was confirmed with a quick awkward glance.

Lucretia made her way over to the counter, holding out her hand to Steven. "Hello, my name is Lucretia Darknight. It's a pleasure to meet you." The chance meeting felt more like a planned appointment.

"Have we met somewhere before?"

In a sultry tone, she said, "I hardly think so. However, if we had, it must have been a pleasant experience." The diner suddenly got dead silent while the two exchanged conversation.

Steven stammered, "Excuse my ignorance. My name is Steven Spencer."

"Yes, I know who you are. Steven Spencer, the writer? I've read all your books. It's nice to finally meet you." An uncomfortable pause flashed between them.

Lucretia smirked. "Would you please join me at my table?"

The invite seemed the perfect invitation. "Of course, thank you, Ms. Darknight."

"Please, call me Lucia."

They both settled at the table. "That perfume you're wearing; I know it from somewhere."

"You seem to be familiar with a lot of things about me, Mr. Spencer," she scoffed. "The scent is called sweet peppermint. I have an aromatherapist mix it special for me."

"It's definitely unique," Steven replied.

She sighed and continued, "I couldn't help hearing you mention Branchview. I happen to be an employee of Branch Consolidated Industries."

"I'll go out on a limb here, and guess that Branchview is the residence of the Branch family. No pun intended." Lucretia slowly rolled her eyes.

"Oh yes! It's a very large, and very old estate. I actually live in a separate cottage within the property."

"How interesting. I'd like to see this place."

Lucretia replied rather seductively, "My cottage, or the main house?"

Steven reacted with subtle embarrassment. "The main house, of course." He paused. "I'm sure your cottage is very nice as well," Steven stammered. He felt an uncomfortable energy talking about this kind of thing with any women except Loraine.

She said with a haunting smile, "Perhaps you can stop by and see it some time?" She paused to gauge his uncomfortable reaction. "I can take you to the main house if you'd like. I'm sure the Branch family would be more than interested in meeting a great writer such as yourself."

"I appreciate the invitation." She glared across the table with daringly seductive eyes.

Steven replied with an uneasy smile.

"Great, I will make the arrangements, and you can call me later this afternoon." She handed him a business card. "Until then, Steven…" she smiled.

As Lucretia walked away, she glanced back at Steven with such an alluring stare, he nearly crawled under the table. The old man at the counter turned, "Watch out for that one!"

Steven nodded and beckoned to Suzy. "I think I'm ready to order."

She made her way over to the table, "I will have two eggs OE with bacon crisp and rye toast. Oh, and make sure the hash browns are not greasy."

"Of course, is that all?" she asked.

"Oh, some more coffee, please. And since no one took my vacant seat, I'll move back over to the counter." Suzie smiled.

Steven finished his breakfast and paid with a generous tip for Suzie. He decided to take a drive before meeting up with Lucretia. He was anxious to see if any sights might trigger a subliminal memory from any of his dreams. It was a nice little town, not much different than others along the New England coast. The inhabitants still waved an American flag outside their small shops and businesses, and it had excellent views of the Atlantic in its recently refurbished harbor district. There were also lots of monuments marking its rich history. Steven called Lucretia and agreed to meet her at the harbor viewing area at 3:30.

By the time Lucretia pulled up next to him in her black BMW sedan, and seductively motioned for him to follow, a late afternoon mist had rolled in. It was a common weather pattern for the cold Atlantic area. It added even more to the allure of the small unknown town that was home to the mysterious Branchview Estate.

When Steven and Lucretia arrived at the estate, they strolled up the walkway through a thick fog in a manner that was eerily familiar.

Seated in the middle of the wooden doors was a large, brass lion head knocker. "The fog seems to be coming in a bit early today," Steven attempted to make small talk. "Oh, that is quite a chill in the air." Lucretia smiled.

"I am sure the weather is much colder than in Florida." Steven looked puzzled.

"How-" he paused. "Never mind…" Steven sighed with amazement. "This is all quite uncanny. Everything is just as I'd envisioned it."

Lucretia gave an almost all-knowing smile, then grabbed hold of the large ring in the lion's mouth, and banged it loudly against the door. After a few moments, the echo of heels on the tile floor could be heard casually clicking from the interior. The sound suddenly stopped as Penelope Locke Branch, a well-maintained, regal woman in her mid-70s opened the door and stood firmly in the entryway.

"Well hello, Lucia! What a splendid surprise."

"Hello, Mrs. Branch. I brought a very special guest here to Branchview." Penelope reacted with shock as she laid eyes on Steven.

In an instant, her balance faltered, and Penelope exhaled a terrified breath. "Mrs. Branchview, are you alright?" She nodded.

"Thank you, dear," she whispered.

"Do you need some help?" Steven asked. The two women shook their heads.

"Thank you, Steven, I can help her," Lucia replied.

Steven paused to inspect the interior of the grand old estate. Seated just adjacent to the foyer was Daniel Branch III, a properly well-groomed man in his mid-40s. It seemed odd that the man never faltered in his stance, just continued to sip on his brandy.

"Are you alright, Mrs. Branch? You look as though you've seen a ghost."

Penelope recovered somewhat and glanced once again toward Steven. "I apologize for my reaction. It's just…" her voice silenced.

Daniel interrupted with an old New England accent, "…that you greatly resemble my late uncle Jack." Daniel strolled closer, eyeing Steven with amazement.

"This is Steven Spencer. We met at The City Diner this afternoon."

"Ah yes! The great novelist, Steven Spencer. I've heard about you."

"I'm greatly flattered."

"Excuse my rude behavior. My name is Daniel Branch III, and this fine woman is my mother, Penelope Locke Branch." They all nodded at each other.

Penelope asked in a softened tone, "Since formal introductions are out of the way, shall we all go to the sitting room?"

"I'll have to pass on that invitation, Mrs. Branch. I have quite a few issues that need my attention this afternoon."

"I understand, Lucia. I hope you come to see us again when you can stay longer." She gave a respectful nod to Mrs. Branch.

"Goodbye Lucia, and thanks for your help," Steven stated.

Lucia replied, in a low sultry voice and with hypnotic eyes, "It was my pleasure, Mr. Spencer. I do hope to see you again very soon." Her connotation caught Steven off guard once again.

Steven continued to scan the room for any clues as to the reason for his visit. Penelope eyed him with an expressive smirk as she showed the way to the sitting room. "Please, Steven, come sit over here with me?" Penelope patted the seat next to her.

Daniel strolled over to the bar to pour another glass of brandy. "Care for one, Steven?"

"Um, no I don't drink," he replied.

"Oh! Very well! All the more for me." he commented while raising his glass in a salute.

"She appears to be quite smitten with you, Steven," Penelope stated frankly.

"I would hope not. I'm already involved with someone."

"I should've known. You being a successful, handsome young man." Daniel raised his glass in a toast.

The mantle clock and the foyer clock chimed in unison, four times.

"It appears to be my tea time. Would you care to join me, Mr. Spencer?"

"Of course! Tea and coffee are more my style, Mrs. Branch." Penelope left to grab the tea cart.

Steven sat alone on the settee. "What sort of business brings you to Lockeport?" she called out from the other room.

"Actually, my interest is right here at Branchview."

Daniel chuckled and paced with his drink. "And what on earth, pray tell, would interest you about this old house? Perhaps the inspiration for a new supernatural novel?"

Steven answered as Penelope handed him a cup of tea and sat back down next to him. The lights flickered, and everyone took notice. "I- hope to find that answer myself, Mr. Branch. For the past few months, I've had strange dreams and visions about this place that I can't seem to explain." Both Daniel and Penelope exchanged a quick wide-eyed glance.

Daniel paused his pacing. "That's interesting-" He paused again. "Interesting indeed. From what I understand, you're somewhat of an expert on affairs of the paranormal."

"Yes. I've studied the subject quite extensively."

Daniel sauntered to the window where the now setting sun cast an orange glow into the room, "As you might imagine…" He stopped and turned to look at Steven. "An old house such as this holds many secrets and mysteries. Not to mention, a bevy of lost and wandering souls."

Steven glanced at Penelope. "I'd most definitely bet on that."

"It appears as though the spirit activity here has been, might I say, increasingly stirred over the past few months."

Daniel turned from the window and motioned to Penelope. "Would you be so kind as to elaborate on that point, mother?"

Penelope set her teacup down and nervously joined in the conversation. "Yes- strange incidents have occurred since the sudden death of my husband. It has everyone in the house on edge."

"I am sorry for your loss, but I understand there was another death on the property last week, right?"

"I—" Penelope hesitated. "Oh my! Yes! Poor Mr. McAndrew! No one should have to die in the manner he did."

"Yes! That is quite a tragedy. One of the customers in the diner told me about it."

Daniel spoke up, "Ah! It was a tragedy indeed! It will also cost us a mere fortune to replace that gargoyle fixture on the facade." He slugged down the last of his brandy, while Steven appeared quite perplexed by his less than remorseful comment.

"Perhaps you'd be kind enough to join us for dinner, Steven?"

Steven thought for a moment. "Sure, I would be honored to accept that invitation, Mrs. Branch."

Chapter Three:

Veil of Darkness

The bright sunny day gave way to the alluring night sky. A time when unpredictable things occur under the veil of darkness. Hidden inside a dimly lit room, Lucretia settled in for the evening, her favorite time of day; when the world escapes reality to immerse themselves in make-believe stories told on a glaring digital screen.

A soft sheer curtain covered the living room window, allowing the resident to move around her home freely undetected by onlookers. Lucretia sauntered across the room in her candy apple spike heels, however by the time she reached the bookcase her shoes found their resting spot toward the edge of the handwoven Safavid silk rug. One particular book caught her attention, one that showed slight wear in the crease of the stitched binding.

She examined the cover; there was a unique feel to the antique leather cover that Lucretia found appealing. As her fingers grazed the cover, a smirk flitted across her lips, *Mr. Steven Spencer. You've finally arrived. Meow!*

The familiar sounds of howling in the distance caught her attention. *Oh... yes, my love I am coming...* Her book found a place on the coffee table, and she wandered back to the bookcase for another specimen. She pulled the book out halfway, and the old case moaned as a hidden door opened. Lucretia entered, and disappeared inside as the bookcase slowly closed by itself.

Across the manicured lawn inside the main house, Steven had joined Penelope at the elegant antique formal dining table. Steven maneuvered his way to the end of the table and pulled the chair for the lady of the house. "Thank you, Steven, my aren't you the gentleman." She smiled.

"Yes, ma'am, I was raised well."

As Steven returned to his seat, Daniel III and his wife Audrey entered the room for dinner. Audrey appeared to have been a beautiful woman at one time, however, the sadness in her soul had aged her face by many years. Behind her entered Daniel IV, a spry ten-year-old with wire-rim glasses, and a disheveled mop of sandy brown hair. Then along came a cute blonde in her late teens, with a hyperactive personality. Heather plopped down in her chair, leaned forward, rested her face in her palms, and stared across the table at Steven.

"Mr. Spencer is so handsome. I can't get over how much he resembles the picture of uncle Jack."

"Now, Heather!" Daniel III announced. "It's not polite for a proper young woman like yourself to make such flirtatious remarks to our house guest."

She rolled her eyes, mocking her father. "I'm just trying to make conversation."

During the meal, everyone's attention was altered as the foghorn bellowed from the nearby lighthouse. Steven looked alarmed. "That's from the lighthouse near the far end of the property," Penelope explained.

"It's very difficult for the fishing vessels to find their way into the harbor on a ghastly night like this," Daniel III added.

"The ghost of the old harbormaster will help them," Daniel IV announced. The table chuckled.

"Oh really, Daniel! You don't believe that old worn-out tale now, do you?" his father asked.

"It's true, Dad. I've seen him near the lighthouse." Daniel III glanced down the table to catch Steven's reaction to the conversation.

"The boy most definitely has an overactive imagination." Steven ignored the comment and peered across the table at Daniel Jr.

"I believe you, Daniel," Steven said. "I'd like to hear more about it sometime." Everyone paused awkwardly, and Daniel Jr appeared pleased by Steven's interest.

Audrey perked up. "Why shouldn't we believe him? If ghosts exist within these walls, why shouldn't they exist outside as well?" The family exchanged awkward glances.

Daniel Jr put his fork down. "I don't feel much like eating right now. Can I go watch TV, and eat the rest later?"

"Have you-?" his father started.

Audrey interrupted, "Yes you may!" Daniel cast a stern look toward his wife; the scenario grew tense as Daniel Jr departed the room.

"Well, if he can go, then I want to go as well," Heather demanded. "I have a phone call I need to make."

Daniel Sr gave her a quick nod. "Children can be a challenge sometimes."

In the distance, the dogs could be heard howling outside. Audrey slammed her fork onto the antique dining room table. "I wish those damn dogs would shut up. I can't stand it anymore."

Daniel Sr. replied, "I must agree, Audrey. They are very annoying."

"They've howled like that every night since..." Steven noticed her pause. He saw her husband insisted she stop with one glance. In frustration, Audrey bolted from the room, creating a rather awkward scenario.

"Well! I guess that leaves us as the sole survivors of the dinner table." Daniel stated.

"I must apologize for Audrey's behavior, Mr. Spencer. The activity in this house has caused great stress as of late."

"I can fully understand. Dealing with paranormal phenomena can be very unnerving."

Penelope sighed a breath of anxiety. "It's an amazing coincidence that a paranormal expert such as yourself would show up, just as all this is taking place. Do you think there is anything you could do to help us?"

Daniel Sr quickly added, "We'd be willing to pay you generously if you could help restore even an ounce of normalcy to this place."

"This may sound crazy, Daniel… but I think I'm supposed to be here anyway. Yes, I most definitely would like to help in any way that I can."

"Have you by chance secured accommodations in town?" Penelope asked.

"To be truthful, I haven't. I had no idea what to expect or if anything might come of this trip."

"Well… Steven," Penelope announced. "Then we would be delighted if you'd stay here with us for the duration of your visit. I can have the maid prepare a room for you in the north wing."

"Most certainly! We wouldn't accept any other answer but yes," Daniel Sr stated.

"Very well then I guess it settled. I most graciously accept."

Chapter Four:

Back in Florida

Back in Florida, lost deep in her latest novel, Loraine was typing away on her Apple desktop. Mrs. Porter moved silently into the room and startled her. "I'm—" she paused.

"Oh, you scared me!" Loraine announced.

"I'm sorry, do you need anything before I turn in for the night?"

"No… I am good." She removed her glasses to rub her eyes. "I should be calling it a night myself very soon."

"Have you heard anything from Mr. Spencer?"

"He only texted me about arriving safely, but I'm quite confident that all is well."

Mrs. Porter looked anxious. "I wish I could be so sure myself."

"You worry far too much. Please go, and sleep well, my dear."

"Well, I will worry for both of us, then. Something is amiss. But, nevertheless, goodnight, and I'll see you in the morning." She closed the door and let Loraine continue her work.

Loraine took a deep breath and resumed reading her last paragraph. *Oh finally…* she muttered. When suddenly, the door burst open; she heard heavy breathing in the hallway. "Hello… Is there someone there? Mrs. Porter? Bumpers?" A cool breeze swept through the air and Loraine got an uneasy feeling.

As she leaned back into her chair, the light on her computer screen flickered. The incident caused her some concern. She sat forward as the monitor came up brighter. *What…* There seemed to be misspelled words across the page. In the next few seconds, the letters rearranged to spell out the words of a sentence: *Steven is in danger. Hurry… William 'Jack' Branch.*

Loraine cupped her hands across her mouth in horror. *Mrs. Porter was right…*

She glanced away from the computer screen and looked around the room. *William Branch? Who are you?* Loraine was startled once again when the door suddenly slammed closed. Curiosity got the better of her, and she walked over and reopened the door. *Oh… what…? How is this floor wet?* In her stocking feet, she could feel the water soak through her socks, and she noticed the salty smell of the ocean in the air.

Meanwhile, Steven thrashed restlessly in his temporary bed. He was brought to ready when the door creaked and a black cat rushed inside the room. Lucretia suddenly appeared in the dark, dressed in sexy, black lace lingerie. *What…* Steven muttered. As his eyes struggled to see in the dark, he noticed her shadowed body saunter across the room and crawl into bed with him.

The situation caught Steven off guard; he leaned against the pillow as she straddled him. Lucretia had an alluring draw that kept him in some sort of trance. Their eyes locked as she moved closer to his face, ready to seductively kiss him with her serpent tongue. In the distance, the foghorn droned through the night air.

Steven awoke suddenly from his nightmare, only to find himself smack in the middle of another one. Rather than Lucretia, he was looking into the face of a hideous beast leaning over him. The sudden roar coincided with his scream. It was all too much and Steven jolted out of bed, only to see the black cat jump from the bed and scurry out the open door. He desperately tried to gather his senses as the dogs began to howl wildly outside in response to his screams.

As Steven slowly began to regain his composure, an eerie feeling overtook his senses. Nonetheless, he could not shake the notion of being watched. After searching his entire room for digital equipment, it was time to try and get some rest. But he failed to sleep; Steven grabbed his overnight bag and pulled out an old friend. If the house would keep him awake, he decided it was time to do some work. His publisher had been nagging him about completing his latest novel, and that meant reading the manuscript for clarity. Steven could not think of any better time than the present to do such a thing.

Once complete exhaustion took over, Steven finally fell asleep with his laptop open in front of him. At least until the morning commotion overtook the household startling him awake again. *Oh my--*

He heard people shuffling past his bedroom door. The morning had come whether he liked it or not, so it was time to investigate the happenings downstairs. Loraine had trained him well over the years to always make the bed when he got up, which happened to be a nice habit when traveling. Once his quarters were squared away, Steven headed for the breakfast table, however, he got distracted by the intricate wood carving on the banister railing. It was incredible. As he reached the bottom, someone knocked at the front door.

He heard Daniel III yell from the sitting room, "Would someone please answer that door? I'm occupied with a very important call."

Steven shouted back, "I'll get it, Mr. Branch."

He opened the door, and Lucretia greeted him. She was wearing a shiny black rain slicker, "Well! Good morning, Steven. What a pleasant surprise."

"Good morning, Lucia."

She sauntered past him with a dreamy glance. "I trust you slept well last night?"

"As well as possible, I guess…" Lucia looked pleased.

"Ms. Darknight, I thought I heard your voice." Daniel came into the room.

"I thought since it was raining, you might want to ride into work with me today."

He replied, "What a thoughtful gesture. But I'm afraid other business requires my attention, and I won't be in until later."

"Very well then! I'm certain I'll see you sometime later today." Her attention immediately turned to Steven. A seductive glance followed by a long red fingernail up the bottom of his chin. "And I can only hope that I'll see you later as well, Steven?"

She cast an alluring glance as she departed.

"She certainly is a delightful young woman. Don't you think, Steven?"

"A bit too bold for my taste. But I am rather curious. What exactly does she do at your company?"

"Ms. Darknight has only been with us for a few short months, but she's in charge of quality control and corporate scheduling."

Steven was visibly surprised. "I have to say, I didn't expect that answer."

Daniel gave a haughty laugh, "And why not? Could it be because she is, might I say, so sensually alluring, and attractive?"

"I'd call that an understatement."

"It may surprise you to know that Ms. Darknight graduated at the top of her class at Harvard Business School, and she also holds a master's from MIT."

"I'd say that is one very smart woman."

"Very intelligent indeed." Daniel slipped on his raincoat.

"I need to do some preliminary research on the family lineage. Do you have journals?" Steven asked.

"We do, as a matter of fact. You'll find them in the bookcase on your right as you enter the study. They date back to the late sixteen hundred."

"In that case, I guess I have a lot of reading to do."

"Perhaps they'll yield some clues, and help you devise a plan to drive all of the spooks and goblins back into their proper places."

"Perhaps!" Daniel grabbed his briefcase and swiftly headed for the door. "By the way, is there a black cat in the household?"

Daniel turned with a clueless look. "No, but there is a black feral cat that roams the property. My mother puts out food for it from time to time. Why do you ask?"

"It was in my bedroom last night. It jumped off my bed, and ran away when I woke up."

"Impossible! Perhaps it was just a dream. That cat has never been in this house."

"I guarantee it was here last night. I wasn't dreaming."

Daniel seemed perplexed. "I did think I heard a scream last night. Was that you?"

Steven rolled his eyes. "Yes! I apologize. Before seeing the cat, I had a dreadful nightmare."

"No issue. We've gotten quite used to terrifying noises in the night." Daniel pondered further. "I'll make it a point to look into this matter of the cat. Perhaps Daniel Jr brought it inside."

"Perhaps! Kids that age tend to do that sort of thing."

Daniel became anxious. "If you'd be kind enough to excuse me for now, I really need to be going. Please have a very fine day, Mr. Spencer." Daniel departed, leaving Steven in deep thought.

Chapter Five:

My Mother

Steven noted how the conversation with Daniel turned awkward after asking about the black cat. He decided it was time to do some research on the family history. He learned through years of experience it was the best way to understand a family's dynamics. Since there were no other pressing tasks in Steven's day, he passed through the kitchen for some breakfast muffins and coffee, before heading off to the study.

Steven immediately noticed the grand mahogany desk placed in the center of the study. He was always a fanatic of antique furniture. After eating his muffin, he took a few sips of coffee while admiring the incredible library the family had accumulated over the decades. Then one particular book caught his attention. *Oh… yes, this is it.* He dug through the desk drawers and found a pad and pen for note-taking.

The book instantly grabbed Steven's attention, and he lost all track of time reading and taking notes until a sudden cold chill entered the room. *Oh...* He shivered. It grasped his attention just before a crashing roar of lightning flashed outside.

Steven nearly jumped out of his skin. "I have been looking for you all day, Mr. Spencer. I might have known you'd be in here." Penelope entered the room.

Steven was startled. "Mrs. Branch! You caught me off guard."

"Oh, Steven I must apologize. It just gets lonely sometimes in this big house and it's rather nice to have company. Besides, I knew you would not want to be out and about on such a cold rainy day."

"That's quite alright. If you have a moment to sit down, there are a few questions I'd like to ask?"

"Of course!" Penelope settled in a chair near the desk.

"You may want to bring the chair closer." Penelope smiled. "I'm trying to focus on some of the recent histories that might be connected to the increase in paranormal behavior."

"This house has a history of terrifying hauntings, but up until recently we had been enjoying several years of peace." Steven leaned back in the plush desk chair.

"I understand that your husband died here on the property?"

"Yes. He died in that very chair you're sitting in."

Steven reacted rather awkwardly. "I apologize! I can sit in another chair if you'd prefer."

"Oh no! That's quite fine."

He sat forward, less at ease. "Did he have a heart attack?"

"Apparently! Daniel found him with his eyes and mouth wide open, staring toward the ceiling as though he had seen something very terrifying."

"And I understand that it was shortly afterward that all the activity started?"

"Almost immediately! It was as though a portal were open that unleashed all the restless souls from throughout the centuries."

"Can you explain some of the activity?"

She grew tense. "Yes! Strange noises, whispers, apparitions, sudden temperature changes in the rooms, and doors opening, and closing by themselves. And of course, those howling dogs."

Steven jotted down notes, then paused to think. "I'm curious about this Jack Branch that supposedly looks a lot like me."

Penelope's mood suddenly altered; a fond, almost cheerful look covered her face. She stood up, and moved toward the window and stared out as if looking into another world. "He was my husband's brother. William was his name, but he preferred to be called Jack. A wonderful man." She turned back toward Steven. "Unlike the other Branches, he was very trendy, outgoing and everyone liked him."

"I can tell you were very fond of him as well."

"Much more than that, Mr. Spencer." She turned away emotionally. "I was deeply in love with him."

Steven was surprised at the revelation. "But you were married to his brother." She turned back.

"I would've changed that if I only could. My husband was a cruel and vicious man. I'm almost grateful that he's dead." She sat back down, desperately leaned forward, and placed her hand on top of Steven's. "Mr. Spencer, you must not tell the others. Let this be between you and me alone?"

"Whatever is said between us won't go any further, Mrs. Branch." Penelope smiled with relief.

"Thank you, Steven, I am so glad you are here. Maybe we can get to the bottom of the happenings in this house. Now, I've already taken too much of your time. You appear to be very deep in your work." She smiled warmly. He nodded.

Steven stayed in the office quite late, reviewing all the old journals. The maid brought him dinner and checked on him before she retired for the night. Once he returned to his room, the dogs started howling almost right on cue. It was an eerie tone that seemed to carry long into the night. It was almost 3 am before Steven fell asleep. His mind ran wild with computations about the spiritual occurrences in the Branchview Estate.

The next morning, Steven heard the commotion in the hallway. He was not used to being in a house with children. All the distractions had him longing for home. However, he had grown fond of Penelope in a short time and knew she desperately needed his help.

In the dining room, Audrey was sitting at the table drinking coffee, and reading a paperback book. A chilling air stirred, and she clutched the collar of her sweater tighter. "Oh, did you feel that?" she muttered.

The swinging door leading to the kitchen opened slightly, "Martha! Martha! Is that you?" She curiously got up and edged closer to the door. It suddenly flew open as Heather marched into the room wearing a rain jacket.

Audrey collapsed from anxiety onto the end of the table. "Heather! You nearly scared the life out of me."

"I'm sorry, Mother. I didn't mean to."

"Were you out in the kitchen that whole time?

No! Can't you see I'm soaking wet? I went to get the mail, and came in through the back door."

"Was Martha in the kitchen?"

"No… Mom, she hasn't gotten here yet. Is something wrong?" Heather replied.

Audrey stressfully vented, "No! No! Everything is fine, sweetheart."

Heather smacked the mail on the table. "Would it be okay if I went with Andrea Hill and Suzy McVea for dinner at the Mermaid Inn tonight?"

"Heather," her mother stated, "I'm not sure if that's a good idea. The weather is terrible, and I hate the thought of you girls being out by yourselves after dark." She turned away to avoid the conversation. "They haven't found the Norton girls killer yet, and I worry about those wild dogs that have been around."

"Oh, Mother! We'll stay close together, and we'll be in Andrea's car. It's not like we're out walking the dark streets."

Audrey paused in anxious thought. "Have you finished the assignments Mrs. Blakely left for you to do?"

Heather took a deep breath, "Yes. My homework is all caught up."

"Okay! You can go. But I want you back here at the house no later than eight o'clock. Am I clear on that, young lady?"

Heather perked up with excitement, "Yes ma'am!" She kissed her mother on the cheek. "I love you, Mother." She hurried from the room, leaving Audrey with a worried expression.

On his way to the dining room, Steven heard Daniel Jr. conversing with someone in the sitting room and decided to wander in. He saw young Daniel playing with a toy truck. "Hello there, Daniel!"

"Hi, Mr. Spencer!"

Steven knelt on the floor. "Hey… that looks like a Ford truck from the 1970s."

"It's just like the one my uncle Jack drove. The truck is still right where he left it when he died."

"Really… and where would that be?"

"Out in the old carriage house. His Corvette is there too. I can show you if you'd like to see them."

"That would be great, but let's see how the weather is tomorrow. It's rather nasty out there today."

Daniel looked at him with a subtle smile. "Are you here to chase off all the ghosts?"

Steven leaned back and moved to the couch. "I'm going to give it my best shot. Are there quite a few?"

"I see a few. But I only talk with the friendly ones."

Daniel looked tense. "Do they talk back?"

"Sometimes. But Maggie is the only one that talks back all the time. She was just here before you came in."

Steven glanced around the room.

"Wow… and who's this Maggie?"

"She's a girl about my age that lived here a long time ago. She always meets me in the Grand Corridor, and tells me all about my dead relatives."

"The Grand Corridor? Where is that?"

"It's in the south wing where my grandmother stays."

"Daniel!" Audrey yelled from the other room.

Daniel shrugged. "I have to go. I'll talk to you later." He ran from the room, leaving his truck behind.

Something intrigued Steven about the truck, and he decided to look closer after Daniel left. The sight of it gave him the chills. The day flew past, and all seemed to settle down after everyone moved on with their day. Steven went back to the study and took another look at the files. He was certain there were clues among the pages, something to show some answers. However, one thing was for sure: there were many hidden secrets within this family.

Daniel III came home from work for the day and was headed for the sitting room to relax when the door knocker sounded against the giant wooden doors.

"Oh…I should've closed the blasted gates for the night."

He paused for a few seconds, clueless as to who would be knocking on his door on such a dreadful night. As he opened it, a woman holding a dog, and dragging a tote suitcase stood in the doorway.

The storm had turned violent outside. "May I help you?"

She wiped her wet, matted hair from her face. "Hello! I'm here to see Steven Spencer."

A flash of lightning cracked, causing them both to flinch. "Yes! Please do come in before you catch your death of cold." Loraine shuffled in with Bumpers, both shivering from the damp cold.

Daniel acted with urgency. "Please remain here for a moment, and I'll retrieve some towels for you and the dog."

As Daniel hurried from the room, Penelope curiously entered to see what was going on. She halted; a panicked look covered her face; her scream carried throughout the house.

Daniel hurried back clutching towels. "Mother! What on earth is your problem?"

He handed a towel to Loraine and bent down to towel dry the wet dog. Penelope trembled with tears in her eyes as she pointed toward the dog. "Th-- the dog… he looks exactly like Scooter."

Daniel looked up at Loraine. "He was an old beloved family dog. I apologize that my mother reacted in such a fashion."

The scream caught Steven's attention from the study, and he hurried into the foyer. "I heard a scream!" He was shocked to see Loraine and Bumpers. "Lori?" He rushed to first embrace and kiss her, then looked at her with questionable surprise.

"I'll explain later," said Loraine. Daniel IV hurried to pet Bumpers.

"Cool! That's a dog just like uncle Jack had."

Loraine looked at Steven seriously. "How interesting!"

Audrey reacted with stressful annoyance. "Leave the poor dog alone, Daniel. This is no time for play." Daniel IV returned to his mother's side.

Daniel III turned to observe Steven with Loraine. "It's quite obvious that you two are intimately acquainted."

"Yes, Daniel," Steven stated. "I apologize for the confusion. This is Loraine Sandstrom, my writing partner, as well as my life partner."

Daniel held out his hand. "Pleased to meet you, Ms. Sandstrom. I'm Daniel Branch, this is my mother, Penelope Locke Branch, my wife Audrey, and my son Daniel Jr."

"It's very nice to meet all of you. Thank you for letting Steven stay here in your lovely home."

"I'm so embarrassed about my behavior, Ms. Sandstrom. Please settle by the fire in the sitting room, and I'll prepare some hot tea."

"Thank you so much. Would it by chance be possible for Steven and I to have a few moments in private?" Loraine asked.

"Of course," Daniel replied. "We'll close the doors to give you some privacy, and if it's quite all right with you, I'll take the dog and attempt to find him some food in the pantry."

"That's very kind of you, Mr. Branch," Steven replied. The family, with Bumpers, exited the foyer, as Steven and Loraine moved to the sitting room.

Steven hastily ushered Loraine to the fireplace. "What's wrong with you? I can walk very well without your forceful assistance." Without responding, he grabbed a throw blanket from the loveseat and gently wrapped it around her wet body.

In complete dismay, she looked up at Steven, "I-" He bent down and placed a passionate romantic kiss on her lips. "I missed you."

Once he completed his display of affection, Steven sat alongside Loraine next to the warming fire. "Now, tell me! What are you doing here?"

She sputtered, "A message flashed onto my computer screen saying you were in danger. It was followed by a name that was just mentioned in the foyer."

"Who's name?"

"William 'Jack' Branch."

He gave her an all-knowing nod, "That name's been mentioned quite a few times in the past few days. I'm beginning to think he's one of the main reasons we're here."

"I just felt very tingly when you said that. Do you suppose he's trying to tell us something?"

"All that I know so far is that I bear a striking resemblance to him, and now we've learned he had a dog that looked like Bumpers."

"Well, I wasted no time getting the first possible flight. And of course, I wouldn't dare tell Mrs. Porter that I received that message."

Steven laughed. "Good! If she had found out, you very likely would've had a traveling companion."

Loraine curiously glanced around the room. "The Victorian decor is amazing and so romantic."

Steven kissed her again. "Steven!" she smiled. "We're in someone else's house."

"You're right. We should conduct ourselves in a more dignified manner." As he attempted to stand up, Loraine impulsively, and forcibly, pulled him back and kissed him with unbridled sensual vigor.

While the love birds cavorted in the sitting room, the Branch family delightfully hovered over Bumpers, who was devouring his food. Their faces were giddy with joy.

Martha Pinchon, the chef, peered over the looky-loos distraught that a dog was in her kitchen.

Daniel III announced, "There, there! That was one hungry little dog."

"I can't get over how much he looks like Scooter," Penelope stated.

"Could we get a dog?"

"Now Daniel, a dog is a tremendous responsibility. Perhaps we'll discuss that matter at a future time." He looked up at his father sulking with disappointment. "While we're on the subject, Daniel, did you by chance allow that feral cat into the house?"

"No! Dad, no way, I haven't seen it for at least two weeks."

"Interesting! Mr. Spencer claims he saw that cat in his bedroom last night."

"If Daniel says he didn't let it in, I believe him," Audrey said.

Penelope stood with urgency, "Oh dear! I nearly forgot. Martha! Could you please prepare two hot teas, and take them to our guests in the sitting room?"

"Yes, ma'am. I'll do that right away."

Penelope moved closer to Daniel Sr. "Should we show Mr. Spencer the picture of Jack and Scooter that hangs in the Grand Corridor?"

"Perhaps tomorrow, Mother. With the unexpected arrival of Ms. Sandstrom, I don't quite think tonight would be an appropriate time."

"There's never an appropriate time for anything in this house," Audrey quipped.

He replied with a raised eyebrow, "Audrey! Where is Heather tonight?"

"She went to dinner at the Mermaid Inn with her friends."

Daniel appeared peeved. "On a blustery night like this? Need I remind you that she is only seventeen?"

"Yes, and she's old enough for us to start granting her certain freedoms."

At that moment, Daniel's cell phone rang. "Heather! Where are you?"

Her voice was panicked and loud. Barking dogs could be heard in the background. "We're in

Andrea's car. We're stalled out along the side of the road, and there are wild dogs all around us."

"What road, and how far from here?" His tone lowered.

"We're on Old Platt Road, Daddy. Please hurry. We're just a few miles away."

"I'll be right there, sweetheart. Do not get out of that car, and lock the doors."

Audrey saw the fear cover her husband's face. "I want to go with you."

"Absolutely not! You stay here with Daniel Jr. I'm taking my rifle with me to ward off those dogs." Daniel swiftly headed for the utility shed to fetch it.

Steven heard the commotion in the foyer and looked to Loraine with alarm. "What's going on? Did you hear that?" Loraine nodded.

Penelope opened the door to the sitting room, and Steven met her at the entrance. "Is everything alright?"

She looked very worried, "No, Heather's friend's car broke down, and there is a pack of dogs swarming it. Daniel went to get them."

Steven and Loraine glanced at each other. Their minds raced with all sorts of questions.

A few hours later, Penelope and Audrey waited impatiently in the sitting room with Steven and Loraine.

The front door opened, and all rose in anticipation. Heather ran into the room and frantically embraced her mother, as Daniel sauntered in behind. "Oh, Mother! It was terrible! Those dogs were crashing at the windows, and trying to get in."

"It's okay, sweetheart! It's all over now, and you're safe. Let's just go upstairs and get you calmed down." Audrey escorted Heather from the room.

"The other girls! Are they safe?" Penelope pleaded.

"Yes. I drove them home. As you can imagine, they were quite shaken."

"Did you have to shoot any of the dogs?" Steven asked.

"No! It was quite strange. When my headlights shined on the scene, they dispersed and ran off into the brush. It was as though they disappeared." Steven and Loraine exchanged a tense glance.

Penelope sat back down, still trembling with anxiety. "Something has to be done about those dogs. I shudder to think what might have happened if they had been able to penetrate the glass." Daniel noticed Bumpers asleep in front of the fireplace, and his tension eased.

"I see our little friend has made himself at home."

"Sleeping like a baby," Loraine said.

"With all the excitement, I forgot to have the maid prepare a room for you, Ms. Sandstrom."

"Oh! Please don't bother. I had planned to room with Steven."

"Oh! I see! When you mentioned you were life partners, did that also mean you are married?"

"No, not technically. We simply have a special domestic arrangement."

"Ah! How modernistic!"

"Yes. After all, we do live in the twenty-first century," Loraine said. Steven reacted with wide eyes at Loraine's comment. Penelope eyeballed them both with a mischievous smirk.

Across the Branchview Estate, Lucretia was nestled in by her fireplace. She gazed hypnotically at the hot orange flames.

While Steven and Loraine bid the family goodnight and headed for their room. The only place Loraine had any intention of staying was with Steven. The whole night had set her nerves on edge.

Bumpers followed close behind as they ascended the stairs. He took a spot at the end of the bed. Loraine sat on the edge, gathering her night items when a cold chill swept through the room. She turned to look at Steven with surprise. "These old houses tend to be so drafty. I'm not used to the cold."

Steven motioned to crawl under the covers, "That means we'll just have to snuggle a little bit closer."

Loraine suddenly felt the tension in her temples. "Ah…" she flinched. Steven also noticed the energy change.

Bumpers moved closer to Loraine in a protective stance, with a guttural growl. All of a sudden, he flew to the door, barking loudly. "There's some sort of force that is trying to get into this room. I must try to block it." She stared firmly, and intently at the door which was now slightly shaking, as the doorknob started to turn. Loraine extended her hands toward the door. "Whatever you are, I block you with the powers of all that is good." Almost immediately, everything calmed. Loraine collapsed against the headboard with a deep sigh. Bumpers headed back to the bed and took his place at her feet. "Whatever was trying to get in this room was a very powerful force."

Steven nodded. "You have no idea. I hope that's the last bit of drama we have to deal with tonight." Outside, the dogs immediately began their howling rant.

"Oh, Steven! What have we gotten ourselves into?"

"I don't know. But somehow, I get the feeling we're not going to be able to walk away until it's resolved." Loraine scooted beneath the covers.

Steven reached up and turned out the lights. He let out a deep sigh. Lucretia flinched as she sat by the fireplace; inside, her frustration turned to rage.

Something… I will find out who's blocking my presence in Steven's room. She walked to the window and stared toward the main house with ambitious intent.

Across the estate, in the Branch family cemetery, a broken silhouette of a man painfully moved with desperation through the torrential rain toward a large mausoleum. *Oh…* he groaned heavily. Soggy seaweed hung, clinging to his flailing limbs. The fog horn desperately droned through the night air from the nearby lighthouse. An eerie creak resonated when he opened the entrance gate. He limped inside, and reached his weathered hand toward the granite stone marker with a name carved on it, 'William Jack Branch February 6, 1943 – June 14, 1978.'

Chapter Six:

The Mysterious Ms. Darknight

The morning sun brought light in the wake of the previous night's turbulent storm. The new day brought more familiarity and clarity of mind to seek the promise of finding a new piece to the puzzle. Loraine found determination for the reason they had been sent to the Branchview Estate.

In the sitting room after breakfast, Loraine sat comfortably on the loveseat sipping on a cup of coffee. After the long grueling night, the hot beverage worked to awaken her sleepy body. Bumpers found a nice place to rest next to his caretaker.

"Good morning Ms. Sandstrom," Daniel III announced.

"Good morning to you as well, Mr. Branch."

"I trust you slept well last night?"

"We had a slight incident, but nothing that couldn't be handled. Has your daughter recovered from her ordeal?"

"She's still sleeping. I couldn't bring myself to wake her up."

Daniel strolled over to the side table and poured a glass of brandy. "Where is Mr. Spencer, still sleeping?"

"No… as a matter of fact, he got up at the crack of dawn and drove to Boston to purchase supplies."

"Oh…" Daniel wandered over to the loveseat. "Good morning Bumpers." He scratched his ears. "Couldn't he have obtained the supplies here in Lockeport, or perhaps New Haven?"

"I'm afraid not. I had to send him to a particular metaphysical store in Boston that carries all the items I'll need to begin my work."

Daniel paced toward the window. "I must admit my skepticism about things you define as paranormal-" He paused. "However, I'm willing to give your work the benefit of the doubt in this particular case."

"I assure you that I am very good at what I do."

Daniel turned. "I'm curious about your accent. Are you from Great Britain?"

"Yes… very good. I'm originally from Chelsea."

"I know that area quite well. Our descendants are originally from Knights Bridge."

"I couldn't help but notice you speak the King's English as well."

He swirled the brandy in his glass. "Yes. It was passed down through the family for decades, but unfortunately, I'm the last in my lineage to carry the tradition."

A loud knock was heard in the other room, pausing Loraine's response. "I wonder who that might be?" Daniel swiftly departed.

Daniel swung the door open.

"Daniel…" Lucretia swept past him, without invitation.

Her presence caught him off guard. "Good morning, Ms. Darknight. Should I assume you're here to offer me a ride to work?"

"I had hoped… I might be able to see Mr. Spencer."

Daniel closed the door. "I'm afraid that won't be possible. Mr. Spencer has traveled to Boston for the day. Could I perhaps give him a message?"

Lucretia frowned. "I was hoping he would join me for dinner at the Mermaid Inn this evening."

Loraine heard the conversation and made her way to the foyer. "I'm afraid that won't be possible either."

Lucretia responded with ire. "Really! And who exactly are you?"

"I'm Mr. Spencer's significant other."

"I wasn't aware that he was married."

"He and I have what you might call… a domestic arrangement."

Daniel uncomfortably interrupted. "Lucretia! This is Loraine Sandstrom."

He then turned to Loraine. "This feisty young woman is Lucretia Darknight, one of my employees."

Lucretia held out a limp hand. "Oh yes! The famous writer, and notorious White Witch."

Loraine stood firm with crossed arms, refusing to shake her hand. "I prefer the title, practitioner of white magic."

Daniel found the conversation uncomfortable. "If you fine ladies would excuse me, I need to make a very important phone call." The two women stood fast, staring at each other intently.

Daniel awkwardly exited the room, and Lucretia took notice of Bumpers at Loraine's feet. "What an adorable little dog."

Bumpers growled, and promptly returned to the sitting room away from the line of fire. "I guess he didn't like me."

"Animals have a keener sense than us humans."

Lucretia responded with an arrogant smirk. "It was a pleasure to meet you, Ms. Sandstrom. Please tell Steven I dropped by."

"Now that you can count on…" Loraine replied.

Lucretia turned with an unwilling gesture. "You might want to keep your significant other on a short leash. There are plenty of eligible women who would love to get their hooks into a handsome, wealthy gentleman like him."

"No leash would be necessary, Ms. Darknight. He wouldn't have any logical reason for wanting to stray." Lucretia gave a haunting sigh in response.

Loraine knew she struck a nerve with her statement, one that Lucretia could not walk away from. "Well, well, my little British tart. If it's a war you want, it's a war you shall get." Loraine smirked this time.

Lucretia made her way down the main walkway, while Loraine remained firm in her premise. *If Miss Peppermint Spice thinks she can steal Steven away, she'd be best to think otherwise.* She continued to vent her anger softly as she closed the door. *Peppermint! That's the odor that drifted into our room last night. I wonder...*

Loraine was lost in thought when she noticed Bumpers sitting in front of a large double door leading to the south wing. "Bumpers, boy, what's wrong with you?" He whined. "Is there something behind that door?"

Loraine wandered closer and paused. "Maybe we need to have a look?" Suddenly, the door opened on its own accord. "Well now, you go first," she proclaimed. Bumpers proceeded cautiously inside the corridor.

After a short foyer, the corridor opened into a large ballroom with white pillars from floor to ceiling at the entrance of the foyer. The floor was tiled with antique marble, and her eyes followed the ornate wood trim to the vaulted ceiling covered in stained glass skylights. "Bumpers, this place is incredible! It's like we are in a giant palace."

As they meandered through the room, along the far wall was a succession of portraits. Loraine studied the people in the paintings, but then she heard another set of footsteps. They were lightly echoing through the grand corridor, and Bumpers started to whimper.

Loraine turned to see a small ten-year-old girl with old-fashioned clothing. "Hello."

"Well! Hello there! Where on earth did you come from?" The little girl shrugged.

"I'm always here. I like to play in this room." She looked down at Bumpers. "Can I pet your doggie?"

"You surely can, sweetheart. His name is Bumpers." She leaned over and gently pet the dog.

"He looks just like Scooter."

"Scooter? Wasn't that Jack Branch's dog?" The child nodded. "What is your name, little girl?

"My name is Maggie. What's your name?"

"I am Loraine, but you can call me Lori."

"You're very pretty."

"Well thank you, Miss Maggie, and you are very beautiful as well." Maggie giggled. "Do your parents know that you're here?"

Maggie shook her head no; Loraine looked puzzled. "I don't understand." Maggie pointed to the wall.

"Would you like to see Jack's picture?"

"Yes. I very much would."

"This way." She walked across the room. "Right there, that's him."

Loraine gasped, speechless. The painting was a picture of Jack with Scooter sitting next to him.

"Magg-" She turned to see that the little girl was now gone. *Oh... my, Bumpers. Where did she go...?*

She turned her attention back to the painting. "Scooter looks like you, and Jack has a strangely remarkable resemblance to Steven." Bumpers barked.

"Ms. Sandstrom! I thought I heard someone in here."

"Oh… Penelope, you startled me. Pardon my curiosity. The doors were open, Bumpers ran in, and I followed."

"That's strange. I always keep those doors closed."

"I assure you that they opened on their own, Mrs. Branch. I would never intend to intrude on your privacy." Penelope's eyes wandered admirably to Jack's portrait.

"I see you discovered the picture of Jack Branch."

"Yes. The little girl, Maggie, showed it to me."

"Maggie? Where did she go?" Penelope looked stunned.

"I don't know. One minute we were talking, the next I turned, and she was gone."

The room suddenly got very still; Penelope gestured to the wall. "Perhaps now you can see why I nearly fainted when I saw Bumpers."

"I can only imagine how you must have reacted when you saw Steven," Penelope answered with an agreeing laugh. Loraine's eyes swept the room. "This is such an exquisitely opulent room."

Penelope smiled fondly. "Yes. We used to have grand parties here that would last long into the early morning hours. But that was a long, long time ago."

"It must've been a wonderful time."

Penelope broke from her deep thoughts. "You must be very hungry, Ms. Sandstrom. Please come with me, and I'll have Martha fix you something to eat." Loraine noticed the abrupt way she hurried to leave the room. The two women pleasantly departed, and Bumpers tagged along behind them.

"Thank you again for not getting upset about us exploring your home…"

"It is alright dear. This is a big house with many secrets." Loraine nodded. "Please… eat. I will see you later."

Loraine entered the dining room, shortly after Heather wearily dragged herself to the table. "Well! Good morning, Heather."

She replied rather squinty-eyed. "I saw you last night in the sitting room."

"Yes, you did. Under the circumstances, it was understandable that we weren't formally introduced. My name is Loraine Sandstrom. I'm Steven's partner."

Heather's eyes widened with interest. "Lucky you! Mr. Spencer is such a hunk."

"It seems that way, as some others have also informed me this morning." They both laughed.

"Oh…" Heather grimaced and rubbed her temples. "I have the worst headache."

"That's understandable, considering the traumatic ordeal that you experienced."

Heather replied emotionally, "It was horrible! I can't get those evil-looking dogs out of my mind. They weren't like any that I've ever seen."

Loraine looked at her curiously. "What exactly did they look like?"

"I don't think I will ever forget the way they looked. There were three of them with thick black fur, large sharp teeth, and horrible, red glowing eyes."

Loraine interrupted. "I imagine how scared you must have been."

"But that was not the worst… They smelled like burnt sulfur." Loraine moved to comfort Heather. "Suzie and I couldn't stand looking at them, but Andrea just sat there staring straight at them as though she were in some sort of a trance."

"It's over with now. I must apologize for putting you through it all over again. I didn't mean to upset you."

Heather settled a bit. "It's okay, Ms. Sandstrom. It's probably best for me not to hold it in, but I should apologize to you for overreacting to your question."

"No apologies needed, but I would advise that you not speak of this to anyone outside the house, and especially not to your little brother."

Heather replied with a pursed smile. "I'm absolutely starved. I need to get a cup of coffee, and have Martha fix me something I can take upstairs to my room."

"It was a pleasure to finally meet you, and I look forward to having future conversations that are of a bit more enjoyable nature."

"I fully agree with that." She nodded.

Loraine contemplated her recent conversation. In light of the news, the situation at the Branchview Estate was much worse than she hoped. Martha brought out some breakfast, and a few minutes later brought another hot cup of coffee.

Chapter Seven:

An Apparition

In the sitting room, an uplifting tune from the ornate ballerina box played, serenading Penelope who was standing near the fireplace. She was entranced by the music.

Daniel III swiftly moved into the room, intruding on her delight. "I'm glad to see that all the furniture in the foyer is still intact."

Penelope closed the music box and turned. "What on earth is that supposed to mean?"

Daniel strolled over and poured a brandy. "I was fortunate enough to escape a pending catfight between Ms. Darknight, and Ms. Sandstrom."

"We should have known that was inevitable. Lucia has definitely set her sights on Mr. Spencer."

"We'll have to find a way of gracefully keeping them apart." Daniel moved gently across the room, "I haven't heard you listen to that music box for quite some time."

"Too long, perhaps." She turned, and carefully placed the music box on the table. "Ms. Sandstrom saw Maggie in the grand corridor."

"Well… I guess Daniel Jr was telling the truth. She has returned after all these years."

"Apparently. But I'm clueless as to the reason why."

"I guess…" Daniel looked out the window. "We better add that to the ever-growing lists of mysteries within this house."

"Why would she choose Daniel Jr and Ms. Sandstrom, and appear to no one else?"

"I don't know, Mother. I wish that I had a logical answer." He chugged down the last bit of brandy and pensively stared out the window. "I see Steven has returned from his day in the city."

Steven entered, carrying a large box of items, and shivering from the cold. "Hello…" he called out. Loraine eagerly entered the foyer.

"I'm so glad you're back. I was beginning to worry about you."

Steven sighed. "It's been a long day, but I was able to get everything done on the list. It's freezing out there!" They exchanged a quick kiss.

"One of the first things we'll have to do is light a reverse candle in our bedroom to keep out whatever was trying to get in last night."

"I picked up five of them, so we have enough to last for a while."

"You're a dear. Were you able to speak with Dr. Grayson?"

"Yes. She was very interested in what I had to say. As a matter of fact, she's on sabbatical until next year, and said she'd be willing to help if her services are needed."

"After the day I had, that just might be necessary," she whispered.

"Why?" Loraine nudged him to keep his voice down. "What happened?"

Loraine looked around, "I actually saw a full-body apparition of a little girl in the grand corridor."

"What-- are you sure?" Steven listened with great interest. "She spoke with me, then showed me a painted portrait of Jack Branch, and his dog Scooter." She rolled her eyes in disbelief. "Steven! The resemblance to you and Bumpers is uncanny." They paused while the grandfather clock chimed. "And there's much more."

"In that case, let's go into the sitting room. I'm dead tired."

"Well, the traveler has returned," Daniel quipped.

Penelope gently hooked Daniel by the arm. "Yes, and I'm quite sure he and Lori would like to have some quality time before supper."

Penelope winked at both of them as she led Daniel from the room.

Loraine moved swiftly to the loveseat and patted the place next to her for Steven to sit.

"I also talked to Heather about her incident with those wild dogs."

"I imagine that was rather terrifying for her to recant."

She leaned in. "By the way—" she whispered. "She described them, and I believe they may be Hell Hounds."

"Hell Hounds!" Steven screeched. "If so, they'd have to be summoned here by a very powerful witch or warlock, and they'd have to enter from some portal that leads directly to hell. Why would they be here in Lockeport?"

"I haven't a clue. But I am convinced that we most certainly are dealing with a profoundly dark, and powerfully evil force." They both leaned back in deep thought. "Speaking of evil forces, your peppermint sweetheart, Ms. Darknight, came by looking for you this morning. Wasn't she the little trollop you had steamy sex within your dreams?"

Steven rolled his eyes. "We didn't have sex."

"Oh really, Steven! It's quite alright. I have those dreams from time to time."

Irritation covered his face. "What did she want? "

"She had hoped to invite you to dinner at a local establishment called the Mermaid Inn."

"Is that so? I have a feeling that woman is going to be a real problem."

Loraine nodded in agreement. "I have to say that I loathe that woman's personality, but I must admit, she is strikingly beautiful. I wouldn't blame you if you succumbed to her charms."

Steven scoffed. "You don't have a thing to worry about. I'm not interested."

"Oh, come now, sweetheart. Any man in his right mind would be enticed by an exotic woman like that."

Steven grabbed her by the shoulders. "Look! I might be sorry for saying this, but I've wanted to say it for a very long time. It's just a phrase that I'm afraid of using."

"What on earth are you trying to say?"

He struggled to swallow. "I love you, Lori! And I have no desire to be with anyone else. There, I've said it!" The statement caught her completely off guard, as Steven never got so serious. It left her speechless. "So, I suppose I've just ruined everything?"

Loraine caught her breath. "On the contrary, Steven. I must admit that I'm very much in love with you as well, and I have been for a very long time."

"Why didn't you ever tell me?"

She rolled her eyes. "Because I feared you wouldn't harbor the same feelings for me."

Steven cupped her cheekbones. "Looks like we just blazed a new trail here tonight."

"Absolutely! I'm overwhelmed." They kissed.

The door pushed open, and Daniel III entered. "Oh, pardon the intrusion, once again. We seem to be out of brandy in the dining room." He motioned toward the bar. "Would you mind?"

"Have at it." Daniel hastened to grab the brandy bottle and promptly poured himself a glass.

"That's a dreadful drive between here and Boston. I'm quite pleased that I don't have to do it myself very often." He turned. "I already know that Mr. Spencer doesn't partake. But would you care to join me in a drink, Ms. Sandstrom?"

Loraine looked at Steven. "Perhaps just a pinch. Thank you."

"I understand," he said as he handed her the glass, "that you had an encounter with one of our resident young ladies earlier today. A ghostly encounter."

Loraine seemed quite surprised. "Yes. It was quite a remarkable experience."

He took a sip of his brandy and fondly reminisced. "I used to see Maggie quite often when I was a child, but it's been many years since she's shown herself. I'm quite convinced that something must have occurred that has disturbed her eternal rest."

"Perhaps that might be true for the other departed souls that reside here as well."

Daniel belted down his brandy. "If you're quite ready, please join us in the dining room. Dinner should be served shortly."

"Thank you, Mr. Branch." Daniel nodded and sauntered toward the foyer. His stride was paused when the dogs began to howl outside. He turned to look at Steven and Loraine.

"Those blasted hounds!" Daniel continued from the room, and Loraine looked to Steven with urgency. "I fear for Heather's friend, Andrea. She mentioned that she had stared directly at the dogs."

"That could be a fatal mistake for her."

"Agreed! We must ensure that she is safe until we can find a way to send them back to the hell hole they came from."

Steven responded, "I fully agree. Well, honey… Let's not keep the Branches waiting."

In the dark of night, at the Branchview cottage, Jeff Manus, a well-built man in his early 20s with dark features, nervously knocked on the mahogany door. Lucretia answered. "It took you long enough to get here. Did you park your car out of sight?"

"Yes… I parked behind that row of pine trees just north of your cottage. What is it that's so important?"

Lucretia turned, pacing away from Jeff. "As you well know, there is a full moon on Friday."

"I didn't need to come all the way over here to be reminded of that tragic fact. And yes, I will be here so that you can lock, and chain me in the basement."

"I see -" she paused to move closer. "I see you've grown wiser since the tragedy you incurred last month."

"I had—" his voice turned angry. "You cannot blame me… I had no idea what I was doing. You're responsible for what happened to Kim."

"Need I remind you that Miss Norton's blood was all over you when you returned to the cottage that morning?"

He turned away emotionally. "I loved her. You turned me into this horrible monster. It's all your fault."

"My dear Jeffrey. How can you say that? You fell into my trap quite willingly. Like all men, you have no self-control where beautiful women are concerned."

"Don't play that game with me, Lucretia. You seduced me! I should kill you, and send you back to hell where you belong."

"Why would you want to kill the only person who can cure you of your dire affliction?"

"You'll never cure me. You're too wicked. So, just get to the point of why I'm here."

"I--" she turned to move closer. Jeff could smell her intoxicating perfume. "I have an agenda that must be carried out, and someone has been foolish enough to get in my way."

"What does that have to do with me?" Jeff asked.

Lucretia chuckled. "You're going to help me remove this obstacle."

Jeff defiantly shook his head. "No! I'm not going to kill again for you, or anyone. I refuse to be a part of this."

"I'm afraid you don't have any choice in the matter. I decide whether you kill or not."

The lure caught Jeff hook line and sinker; he surrendered. "Please! I just pray that it's not someone I know."

She smirked, and strolled closer, shaking her head. "You don't know her. She's a White Witch with powers equal to mine, but she'll never expect that I have a secret weapon."

"Well… what's her name? Wait! Don't tell me. It will make it harder."

A wicked smile crossed her face. "I'll tell you anyway. Her name is Loraine Sandstrom."

Chapter Eight:

The Mysterious Message

A mysterious message scrolling across the computer screen had brought Steven to a magnificent, historic home full of tales. The Branchview Estate was once a warm, inviting, luxurious home for a beloved family. Amid a surprising battle brewing beneath the depths of the human psyche, a couple found love in each other once again.

The first blanket of snow had covered the lush green lawn at Branchview. Steven and Loraine rushed outside to lob snowballs at each other, rejoicing in the crisp winter air. Behind the scenes, they were working diligently to forget the horror that was about to befall the Branch family.

"Oh… yes! I gotcha!" Loraine shouted. Steven laughed.

He rushed to her side, embracing his loved one as they fell back into the snowmaking angels like school children.

"This is absolutely wonderful… it's been too long since we just had silly fun." Steven shivered from the cold.

"I agree. But I can't help thinking that if we were back in Florida, we'd be having coffee by the pool right about now. On a warm 80-degree morning."

"Yes, I suppose you're right. But for the time being, we'll just have to settle for hot cocoa by the fire." Steven leaned in for a quick kiss.

"Well, I don't know about you, but I am ready for that hot cocoa," Loraine quipped.

"Yes, your lips are cold." He giggled. "I'll race you…"

Steven took off toward the house, with Loraine right on his heels. "Come on old man. Is that the best you got?" she said as she passed him by.

The two raced to touch the large mahogany front doors. "Yes!" Loraine announced. "I beat you by a nose." Steven rolled his eyes.

He reached to open the door for her. "My lady…"
She nodded. "Since you were declared the winner, I will
fetch the hot cocoa."

"I like the way you think, mister."

"Just go…"

Steven smirked. Loraine rushed to take off her coat
and headed for the giant fireplace. Steven followed shortly
after. She looked around the room, admiring the grandeur
of the building. It was marvelous, but she could never
envision it replacing their home in Florida.

Loraine turned around when she heard footsteps
across the tile floor. "Oh, bless you, sweetheart." Steven
handed her a large cup of hot cocoa.

They giggled between themselves when Steven
heard someone else enter the room. "Good morning Miss
Penelope."

"There you are, you two. We missed you at
breakfast."

"We got up early and did not want to wake anyone,
so we went to the City Diner." Penelope smiled.

"Loraine, would you mind if I had a word with Steven? I'd like to show him the picture of Jack Branch in the Grand Corridor."

"Absolutely! In fact, I had hoped to speak with Audrey and Heather this morning."

"Then you're in luck. They're both in the dining room with Daniel Jr." Loraine held up her empty cup.

"Very well then. I'll get another cup of this yummy hot cocoa, and join them. I will see you two later."

She departed the room. "Such a charming girl. You're a very lucky young man." Penelope flashed a pleasantly warm smile at Steven. "Follow me, if you will." Steven obliged.

They entered the south wing, and Steven admired the ornate architecture.

"This is a spectacular house, Penelope…"

"Thank you, Steven. I can't wait to show you this room."

Penelope led the way, and Steven was awestruck by the enormity of the room.

"This is one of my favorite places in the house. I spend much time here meditating."

They continued to stroll. "Are all these portraits members of the Branch family?"

Steven paused in front of one particular portrait. "Yes. That one is me when I was a young woman."

Steven smiled. "If you don't mind me saying, Mrs. Branch, you were -" he paused. "I mean, you still are lovely."

"You're far too kind." She blushed.

Steven noticed the painting next to Penelope's. A stern-faced man holding an open book. "That's my late husband, Daniel Branch II."

"Pardon my judgment," he looked at the painting. "But I can sense that he possesses all the unpleasant qualities you previously told me about."

"And then some. You have no idea."

Steven strolled to the next portrait to the far right, "There is no denying who this guy is. If I didn't know any better, I'd swear that was me and Bumpers."

With a weak smile, Penelope sat down in front of the painting. "Your personalities are also quite similar."

She stared admirably at the picture. "Can you tell me more about him, Mrs. Branch?"

Penelope drew a deep breath. "He was so interesting. I could sit and talk with him for hours. Just his intelligence alone could keep me entranced forever."

"I am curious… If you don't mind, how did he die?"

She shook her head and took a deep breath. "There was a problem in one of the factories in Hong Kong…" She stopped to draw back the tears. "Normally, Daniel would've gone, but he decided to send Jack instead. The plane he was on went down somewhere over the Pacific, and the wreckage was never found."

Penelope turned to look at Steven. "Did you hear that?" Steven nodded.

The room suddenly filled with a child's laughter. A little voice called out, "Penelope! Penelope!" She looked around the room anxiously.

Steven stood up, fearing for Penelope. "Maggie! Is that you? Please come talk to us." A small child suddenly emerged from behind a large white pillar. Steven smiled. He looked at Penelope and noticed the tears streaming down her cheeks. "I can't believe you came back after all this time."

Maggie looked at Steven, then pointed toward him. "So, did he."

"Oh, Maggie! That's not Jack. This young man's name is Steven."

"Yes… I know. The other spirits told me of him." Penelope and Steven both turned and looked at each other in disbelief.

Steven asked, "There are other spirits here among us?" The little girl nodded.

"I came to warn you about Charlotte. She's back, and she has evil plans for everyone at Branchview." Penelope looked terrified.

"Whose Charlotte?" he whispered in Penelope's ear.

"She was my twin sister."

"Don't worry, others will come back, and many will be here to help you."

Maggie turned quickly and looked toward the back of the room. "I have to go—" Penelope looked sad. "I'll talk to you again very soon." The little girl turned and disappeared into the shadows.

"Maggie… wait! Don't go!" The tears streamed down her cheeks.

Steven moved closer to comfort her. "We must find Lori right away; you need to tell us everything you can about your sister Charlotte. It's now obvious that she's the root of all the problems here at Branchview."

"Wait! Steven, I must ask you something first." He stopped.

"Did you grow up here in New England?"

"Yes! I grew up on a dairy farm in New Hampshire."

"Can—" she stopped. Steven looked puzzled. "Were you by chance adopted?"

"Yes," he replied. "I was… my parents adopted me from a Presbyterian orphanage in Boston." He looked at Penelope with suspicion, as she took on an expression of enlightenment. "Why are you asking me these things?"

Penelope stared intently at him through tear-filled eyes. "Because I..." she stopped. "I think you might be my son."

In that split second, the world stopped. Steven looked at Penelope in complete shock. "What?!" He looked back at her, then over to the picture of Jack on the wall. The eyes in the painting seemed to penetrate his soul.

Chapter Nine:

The Carriage House Secrets

Daniel IV abducted Loraine from her meeting with his mother and sister that morning. It appeared that he had developed a school boy crush on the newest inhabitant of Branchview. He dragged her around by her arm, wanting to show off some of the family's most prized possessions. Inside the large Carriage House garage, covered by a canvas tarp, was a white Corvette in pristine condition.

"Over here, Ms. Sandstrom. You just have to see this!"

"Okay, Daniel okay…" she giggled.

He reached up and turned on the overhead lights. "Isn't it the coolest thing you have ever seen?"

"Yes. It is a very nice car, Daniel."

"Now… come look over here. Gerard is restoring Jack's old truck. Oh, and he takes care of the Corvette as well."

"Really? Whoever this Gerard is, he does a very good job."

"I'll gladly accept that compliment, ma'am."

A very tall, light-skinned black man in his late 40s sauntered out of the shadows.

In a thick New Orleans style French accent, he replied, "My name is Gerard LeRoux."

Daniel quickly intervened. "This is Ms. Sandstrom. She and Mr. Spencer were hired to get rid of our ghosts."

Gerard looked at them with a smirk. "Is that so? And may I ask why you aren't attending to your daily studies with Mrs. Blakely?"

"She gave me a short break."

"Perhaps you should be using that break time to sharpen your math skills. Your father tells me you're lagging a bit behind."

Daniel, annoyed and embarrassed, shrugged. "I just wanted to show Ms. Sandstrom the cars."

"Well, perhaps you should remind Mrs. Blakely that break time isn't until noon."

"Okay! I'll go back to the house. She's probably looking for me right now anyway." He then looked toward Loraine. "I'll see you later, Ms. Sandstrom."

She replied with an assured wink, then turned to Gerard once the boy had departed.

"You were a bit hard on him, weren't you?"

"He's the only one to carry on the Branch name. We must make sure he gets the best education possible."

"Why should that matter to you? He's not your child."

"With all due respect Ms. Sandstrom, we are all like family here at Branchview. I'm Mr. Branch's corporate assistant, and I'm also married to Sharie."

"The housekeeper?"

"Yes. Her family has been employed by the Branches for four generations."

"I can quite understand your feelings in that case. Our employees are much like family as well."

Gerard smiled and gestured toward the stairs. "Sharie is upstairs right now. Could I invite you up for a visit?"

Loraine shivered. "Yes, that would be nice. I'll simply be happy to be spared from this cold, damp garage."

"Please, ma'am, after you," he directed her to the stairs.

Loraine had a strange notion in the pit of her stomach, *this family is full of secrets.* Gerard opened the door and let Loraine enter before him. She glanced around at the Victorian decor that resembled the main house, only on a much smaller scale.

"Sharie!" he hollered. "We have a visitor."

Sharie entered from the kitchen; an attractive woman in her late 40s. "What a pleasant surprise. I was hoping you'd find the time to visit us, Ms. Sandstrom."

"Yes. We barely had a chance to speak while at the main house."

"Please have a seat. It's quiet here, with no one to disturb us."

Loraine sat down at the ornate antique dining table, joined by Gerard. "Would you care to join us for an early lunch?"

"You're so kind to offer, but I can only stay for a short while."

"Well, can I fix you some hot tea? I was just heating some water. You must be freezing in the cold weather, compared to Florida?"

"Yes, please. A spot of tea would be just grand."

"I'll let my charming husband entertain you while I prepare it." Sharie returned to the kitchen.

"I have to say that your accent is very delightful, Ms. Sandstrom."

"Yours as well Mr. LeRoux. Would you by chance be French Canadian?"

"Yes, I am. I was raised just outside of Montreal."

"I've visited there on a few occasions. It's a marvelous city."

Sharie returned with the tea. "Thank you, Sharie."

"Correct me if I'm wrong, but isn't Sandstrom a Swedish name?"

"Wow… I am impressed, that's correct. My father was a diplomat at the Swedish embassy in London."

"How fascinating! We need to talk more about that sometime."

Sharie interjected, "I understand that you and Mr. Spencer are here to help us with our paranormal issues."

"Yes, I hope so anyway. Is there anything you can tell me that might assist us with our investigation?"

Sharie leaned forward. "I believe there is a lot I can tell you. The last time there was this much disturbance was when I was a child back in the 70s."

"Do you recall what may have been the source of those issues?" Gerard sat quietly and listened.

"Only a few things my mother told me. I do know that Charlotte Locke played a major role in the terrible incidents that took place here during that time."

"Who is Charlotte Locke?"

The disdain rolled off her tongue. "She was Penelope Branch's twin sister, but they weren't alike in any way. Charlotte was a witch, and a very evil one at that."

"Are you saying that she practiced Black Magic?" Sharie nodded.

Sharie glanced at Gerard. "The Locke family had a long history of dabbling in witchcraft and the dark arts. Charlotte lived at the cottage where Ms. Darknight now resides. She burned to death in a fire there back in 1981, amazingly all the problems vanished when she passed away."

"Oh my, was the cottage destroyed by the fire?"

"No. It was contained in the basement. As my mother said, supposedly Charlotte was performing some type of ceremony, and her gown came in contact with the candles. However, I don't believe that is the whole story."

"Sharie and I believe the answer to the present issues lies within the ground beneath that cottage."

"What on earth would make you believe that?"

Gerard took a deep breath and paused for several minutes. "Both the Branch and the Locke family were active helpers in the underground railroad. The main tunnel ran below the cottage and led to a secret entrance just below the cliffs. Boats from their fleet would dock along the beach at night, and carry the slaves to freedom in Canada."

"That's all very interesting, but I fail to see how that's connected to the cottage or the present issues."

Sharie looked at her husband, she looked spooked. "A story was passed down through the generations about a group of twenty slaves that were expected one night, and only one showed up, shivering with fear, and smelling like burnt sulfur. When they asked him, what happened to the others, he explained that a fiery hole had opened up in the tunnel and that a large fire breathing beast consumed everyone but him."

Gerard seemed distraught. "That man was my great, great grandfather."

"How horrible! In my studies, I can only venture to guess what that fiery hole might have been."

"I know exactly what it was," Sharie burst out. "The fiery pits of hell."

"It would seem that way, Sharie."

"We are on the same page, Ms. Sandstrom. A portal exists below that cottage, and Charlotte Locke has somehow returned through it." The room suddenly got very quiet.

Loraine knew for there was some reason she had been led to the garage that day. Maybe it was the same reason they were guided to this place. Nonetheless, whatever was happening, it was sure to turn very bad.

Sharie broke the silence. "Can I get you some more tea Loraine?" She smiled.

"No, thank you. I have some things to do. But speaking with both of you has been very enlightening. It's time that Steven and I had a conversation."

Gerard led Loraine to the door. "Thank you, Ms. Sandstrom. I'm sure we will see you again very soon." She nodded.

Loraine left with an unnerving feeling; it had grown immensely since she had entered the house. It seemed the problems at Branchview ran deeper than she could have ever expected. As she strolled across the snow-filled lawn, her mind ran wild with all the possible complications awaiting them in the coming future.

After consulting with Steven and Penelope over the new revelations, Loraine went directly upstairs to work on the manuscript of her latest novel. The maid brought her a light lunch that she nibbled on as she labored.

The antique grandfather clock in the foyer with Winchester chimes tolled three times and echoed hauntingly throughout the house. It was later than she expected; Steven and the others would be waiting in the dining room for the meeting Penelope had scheduled. She could hear the low muffles of them talking to pass the time until everyone arrived.

Penelope sat at the head of the long patina cherry table; it had an incredible sheen considering its age. Steven was seated to her right; another chair was vacant to the left for Loraine.

"Ah, Loraine! We've been waiting for you, dear."

"I know… Sorry for my tardiness. I was working upstairs in my room and lost track of time."

"It's fine dear, please sit." Loraine nodded. "Audrey… is Daniel Jr in another portion of the house? I wouldn't want him to hear some of the things I have to say."

"He's with Mrs. Blakely. She stayed a few extra hours today to help him with his math."

Heather fidgeted. "Will this take very long? I have other plans."

"I am sorry dear; those plans will just have to wait. What I have to say is of dire importance to all the adults in this family."

"I am not an adult…" She turned to Audrey.

"You should be flattered that your grandmother considers you an adult." Heather rolled her eyes and flopped down in her chair.

"Greetings to all!" Daniel III swept into the room. "Being that I was so abruptly pulled away from my work, I should hope that this meeting is of substantial importance."

"Daniel, can you please take a seat so we can get on with the family meeting?" Daniel suddenly got the same look Heather did a few minutes ago. "Okay, I am here now." He leaned back in his chair.

"I assure you, Daniel. What I have to say is very important." He gestured for her to continue. "Steven, Lori, and I have gathered evidence that the spirit of my sister Charlotte has returned to wreak havoc on the Branch family."

Heather gasped and looked terrified. "Are you sure, Grandma?"

Audrey jumped in, "I knew there was something evil going on in this house."

Daniel interrupted everyone. "Come now… that's total insanity! Aunt Charlotte has been dead for a very long time. What, may I ask, would be her purpose in coming back?"

"Daniel, I understand your skepticism, but you were too young to remember. The hell she and my father brought down on this family was horrifying. They hated the Branch family and vowed revenge right up until their dying breath."

Daniel sarcastically rolled his eyes and looked off into the corner. "Then, pray tell, how are we to arm ourselves against such ghastly spirits?"

"It's quite obvious, Mr. Branch. That's the reason Steven and I were summoned to the house."

"That's right!" Steven jumped in. "And the more information we can gather, the better prepared we can be for whatever she, or any other aggressive spirit, has in store for us."

"The good news is that we also have several other spirit allies that have returned to help us fight against her witchcraft."

"I don't understand… What does all this mean?" Heather asked.

Audrey moved closer to her daughter, while Daniel blurted out, "Nonsense! All this talk about witches and evil spirits is nothing more than a fabricated fairy tale."

"I can assure you, Daniel, you could not be farther from the truth. My sister was truly a witch, and my father was consumed with evil and hate. I endured their dastardly tirade, and can indeed tell you that it was more like living a terrible nightmare." All eyes peered at Daniel, and he cowered to the majority. "There's one more revelation I'd like to make known." All listened attentively. "I've done some investigative work of my own, and concluded that Steven Spencer is, in fact, my son."

The table silenced. "That's preposterous, mother! Surely, I would have known that I had a brother."

She peered at him with serious eyes. "It's true. Jack Branch and I were in love and I planned to divorce your father so that we could be together."

Penelope paused to regain her composure. "After Jack's disappearance, it was revealed that I was pregnant. Your father was furious and refused to raise a bastard child under his roof. He sent me off to Boston for the duration of the pregnancy and demanded that I surrender the child for adoption. That child was indeed Steven. I was so embarrassed and feared for my safety that it was best if I kept it all a secret." Penelope placed her hand on Steven's shoulder. "I'm so sorry, and hope you can find it in your heart to forgive me."

An uncomfortable sense overtook the room when Daniel stood up and defiantly lashed out. "If you'd all excuse me, I've had quite enough shocking news for one day. I am going to the Mermaid Inn for the duration of the evening." He marched from the room, leaving everyone speechless.

The rest of the family strolled out behind Daniel, leaving Steven and Loraine with Penelope. "Are you alright?" Loraine asked.

"No… dear, but I will be. They all need time to process the information. Steven, I am sorry…" She got up and left the room.

Steven looked at Loraine, and she shrugged. "Well! Would you like to take a walk before it gets dark?" She nodded.

As they moved through the house from the dining room, Loraine commented, "I don't think since we've been here that I have heard this house so quiet."

"I agree."

"Are you alright?" she asked as they put on their coats in the foyer.

"No, but let's wait until we leave the house to talk about it."

"Sure," she replied.

Steven opened the door and held it for Loraine as they exited the house.

Later that night, Loraine returned to their room to find Steven lying on the bed, staring at the ceiling, lost in his thoughts.

Loraine closed the door behind her, then placed her purse on the dresser as she set about preparing the room for the long night ahead.

She grabbed the black pepper and sprinkled it under the door, then checked the reverse candle on the dresser. He chuckled. "Don't worry! No evil spirits are getting in here tonight."

She turned to see that he had gotten up, and started changing into his pajamas. She watched him nervously while undressing herself. She then placed her Oralite necklace on the nightstand and crawled under the blankets.

"You're right, Steven. Not even Miss Peppermint Spice."

"Especially not here," he smirked. He leaned over and turned out the light.

"Steven?" He grunted in response. "I'm so happy that you're a part of my life."

He rolled over and gently kissed her cheek. "I love you too." They cuddled for moral support.

It took some time for Loraine to fall asleep; she could not help reviewing the conversation earlier that day. It was startling news, but not as shocking as Steven's. The exhaustion finally took over, and she could hear Steven breathing heavily in a sound sleep. It seemed to lull her off into dreamland.

A short time later, Steven jolted from the bed. He scanned the room, "Steven! Steven!" he heard his name being called.

"Loraine, do you hear that?"

She turned over. "What's wrong with you?"

"I heard someone call my name." Steven grabbed his slippers and turned on the flashlight.

"Steven you're imagining things. No spirits can get in here. Come on back to bed."

"I suppose you're right… maybe it was just a dream."

"Come on honey, it's freezing. Listen to the wind."

Steven pulled his robe tight and headed back toward the bed. "Steven! Come to the graveyard."

A split second later, he marched to the door. "Steven… where are you going?" He did not respond. Loraine gave up and curled up under the covers.

Outside the Branchview house, the wind howled with a sinister moan. Steven made his way downstairs and out the front door. It was as though he'd been placed in a trance. As he passed the hedging alongside the walkway, a black cat jumped from the brush and began to follow from a distance.

The flashlight flickered in the blowing wind as he moved among the dark tombstones, most of them covered in snow. A voice continued speaking, "Go to the mausoleum."

Steven obeyed without hesitation; he flashed the light on the arch over the entrance. It read BRANCH. The gate let out an eerie creak when he pushed it open to walk through.

He spotted the name William "Jack" Branch carved in stone among other Branch family members. On the large sarcophagus, Steven found a lion's head and a ring. A man's voice called out, "Pull the ring."

It was almost welded closed from age and Steven had to pull with force. It creaked but opened. He took a deep breath and cautiously entered the tomb, and the flashlight flickered across a dark figure seated on top of the concrete encasement.

"Amazing! It's just like looking in a mirror," the voice said. Steven shivered. "There's no reason to be afraid. I just wanted to see my son."

"Well, you could have picked a better place. Like inside where it's warm."

"I will in time. The journey was very long and left me weary. When I'm rested, I will make myself known."

Steven took a deep breath. "How did you find your way back here, after all these years? Your body was somewhere beneath the Pacific Ocean?"

"Amphitrite lifted me from my watery grave, and brought me home to my final resting place."

Steven moved closer, "Who is this Amphitrite?

"You'll meet her very soon. She's the red-haired mermaid goddess of the seas."

Steven was amused, "You have to be joking. A mermaid?

"Think about what you want. But believe me, they do exist."

Steven moved across the vacant space between them and sat down. His voice quivered from the cold. "I just learned today that you were my real father."

"I've been watching you from a distance for a very long time. I wish I could've been there for you."

"I had good parents. They gave me a happy life while they were here."

"I know. I've spoken with them on many occasions since they passed into spirit."

"Are they happy?"

Jack gave an assured nod, "I had to bring you here tonight to warn you. There are powerful forces here that wish to come between you and Lori. You must secure your relationship as soon as possible, or they will succeed."

As Steven sat listening to his father, a knock-out, raven-haired beauty, identical to the young portrait of Penelope strolled into the tomb, wearing a long black gown. "Would those evil forces you speak of include me?"

Jack stiffened with anger. "Charlotte!" She paced closer with determined vigor.

"What's wrong, Jack? I thought you'd be happy to see me again. Don't I remind you of what my twin sister used to look like?"

Jack stood. "You could never be like Penny. You're evil to the core."

"Oh, Jack! You're hurting my feelings."

She sauntered over to Steven. "M-E-O-W!" Her black fingernail gently glided beneath his chin. "He looks just like you, Jack. It's such a shame that I have to kill him too. Or perhaps I won't have to. He may die tonight from exposure."

Jack stepped between them. "You leave my son alone or I'll..."

"You'll what, Jack? You'll never be able to match my powers. You're just an old, broken spirit."

"Perhaps! But I'll never rest until I see you burning in hell."

Steven started to speak, but then he heard voices calling him from outside the tomb. "Steven!"

Charlotte turned to him. "Isn't that sweet! Your little family has come looking for you. Perhaps they'll find you before you freeze to death." Charlotte's laugh echoed through the tomb as she faded away into the shadows.

Jack turned to Steven, who was almost unconscious from the cold. "I'll see you again soon, and I'll do everything in my power to protect you and the others." He faded away into the dark.

The voices grew closer, and Steven was startled from his trance. He cried out weakly, "I'm in here."

Chapter Ten:

We are Being Watched

Steven stumbled to the entrance of the tomb inside the mausoleum. His trance had lifted, yet he remembered every word of the experience.

Loraine and Daniel had heard his weakened cry. "Steven, where are you?"

He took a deep breath. "In the mausoleum," he cried out with all of his remaining strength.

"Oh, Steven…" She ran toward his half-frozen body, and Daniel followed, along with Bumpers.

Daniel quickly took off his coat and wrapped it around him. "Come on, we have to get you inside. Can you feel your toes and fingers?" Steven nodded.

"Yes, I am fine. Just need some warmth and sleep. It's been quite a night."

"Yes, and we want to hear all about the events after you have had some rest."

The group marched across the stiff snow, which buckled from the weight of their footsteps. Steven noticed a sharp wind blow past his face as they moved away from the mausoleum. He turned, startled to see a dark figure lurking in the shadows.

He paused. "Steven…" Loraine stopped. "Are you alright? What's wrong?"

"We are being watched…" he whispered. "Don't turn around, I will tell you later. It's best not to alarm the others any more than necessary." Loraine agreed, but Daniel turned to look. "I can't see anything. Perhaps it's just your imagination running wild."

Steven's legs buckled, and Daniel caught him. "I guess I'll have to do this the hard way. In this case, it will be like the rider carrying the horse."

A short time later, Loraine snuggled next to a semi-conscious Steven as they lay in bed once again. Within seconds he was sound asleep. Bumpers jumped on the bed and lay at his feet. Neither one was going to let him leave his side. After Steven went to sleep, Loraine reached over to the nightstand and grabbed some reading material. It was time she did some research to prepare them for what they were facing. She had a gut feeling that it was going to be an epic clash with the supernatural underworld.

Loraine read for hours before Steven woke and began to stir. "What are you reading?" he asked.

"Oh, Steven! Thank heavens you're alright!"

He looked rather perplexed. "Why wouldn't I be?"

"Daniel and I found you nearly frozen to death at Jack Branch's tomb. Don't you remember anything?"

He paused. "I faintly remember talking with Jack in the mausoleum. It was so cold. But I can't remember how I got there."

"Are you saying that he was there?"

"Yes… I would never joke about anything when it comes to the spirit world. And Charlotte...Charlotte Locke. She was there as well. She looked exactly like the painting of Mrs. Branch."

Loraine looked concerned. "What did they say?" Steven looked worried. "This is important…" He nodded.

"He warned me that evil would try to separate you and I. Then Charlotte appeared, and all I can recall is her laugh... her wicked laugh...and the black cat... The same one that was in this room on my first night here."

"We saw that cat as well. He scampered from the tomb just as we entered."

"Oh, wow… I thought it was all a dream." He struggled to sit up. "Why are all these heavy blankets on me?" He looked down. "Why are my feet wrapped in warm towels?"

"Steven, you don't remember, do you? We desperately had to raise your core temperature, and your feet were frostbitten. When we found you in the crypt, you could barely stand, you tried to walk, but Daniel ended up carrying you on his back."

"How did you know where to find me?" Steven stammered.

"Bumpers woke me, and when I got up to look for you, he stood at the front door barking and scratching at it. I knew immediately that something was wrong, so I went to wake up Daniel and we quickly followed your footsteps in the snow."

While Loraine was talking, someone knocked on the bedroom door, then peeked in. "I prepared some more warm towels for his feet," Daniel announced.

"Bless you, Daniel! I can't imagine what I would've done without your help."

"Yes. Thank you, Mr. Branch."

Daniel proceeded to wrap his feet in the warm towels.

"Considering yesterday's revelation, I think it only proper that we start addressing each other on a first-name basis." Steven smiled. "Would you mind if I had a few moments to speak to my brother in private? Boy, that sounds weird…" he added.

"Not at all! I'll go downstairs and prepare some fresh coffee."

"Ah yes! The nectar of the gods. Thank you, sweetheart." Daniel strolled past Loraine with an assuring smile as she left the room.

"I had always hoped to have a brother. But I never dreamed it would be at this stage of my life. I must admit at first it was very upsetting, however, once the shock wore off, it wasn't so bad."

"It took me by surprise as well. Especially considering how I was drawn to this place."

"I must apologize for my behavior in the meeting yesterday. It was completely inappropriate."

"There's no need to explain, Daniel. I can only imagine how you must've felt."

Daniel replied with a friendly smile. "Being that today is Thanksgiving, I savor the opportunity to welcome you and Lori into our family, and look forward to sharing the holiday with you."

Bumpers whined, and Daniel scratched the dog behind its ear. "He was the true hero last night." Both men nodded and smiled at the dog.

"Thank you, brother." They shared a firm, friendly handshake. "When you are ready, we can have a drink or whatever you want in the sitting room before dinner?"

"Thanks, I'll be down in a while. Do you know what time it is?"

"It's already past noon. You had quite a long snooze."

Loraine met Daniel at the door as he was leaving. "Oh, please, you first," he stated.

"Thank you, Daniel," she replied. "I have your precious coffee, Steven."

"Wonderful… it smells divine." He paused to admire her. "Have I told you lately, how beautiful you are?" Loraine blushed.

"You have not… But please tell me now." They both giggled and kissed.

"I am going to freshen up. Are you coming down soon, or do you want to stay in bed for a while?"

"Oh, yes… I can't miss out on my first Thanksgiving with my new family."

"Oh, Steven! If Bumpers hadn't woken me, there wouldn't be anything about this day that would be thankful." He agreed.

Loraine and Steven prepped themselves for the day and headed downstairs to join their long-lost family.

Penelope jumped from her chair when she saw Steven and Loraine walk through the door. "Oh, Steven… I am so glad to see you." She wrapped her arms around him in a grand hug. "I just found you, and I am not ready to lose you again."

Steven smiled. "Well, at least you'd know where to find me—" She pushed his shoulder, "We have to talk more about this experience of yours."

"Yes, we do--- but tomorrow. I want to have a pleasant afternoon with my family." He smiled.

"Okay, Steven, you can't hoard all of Penelope's time," Gerard jokingly stated.

The men shook hands and laughed, while Sharie took Penelope by the arm and ushered her and Loraine to sit on the couch. "It's so good to have the whole family together at the same time."

"Yes, agreed. But I do wish Marcus and Deanna could be here as well."

"It was a tough decision for them, but they decided to stay in Boston and study for their finals."

"But they will come home for Christmas," Sharie paused in mid-conversation when someone knocked at the door.

Penelope got up to answer, but Loraine stopped her. "I can get that, Mrs. Branch."

Loraine moved confidently toward the door. Her demeanor changed once she opened it. "Ms. Darknight, how unexpected."

"Loraine… on the contrary, Daniel was kind enough to invite me." Lucretia pushed her way past Loraine in a bright red coat holding an apple pie.

"How wonderful… please, let me take your coat?"

She grinned. "Certainly." Loraine took her coat; which Lucretia had removed to reveal red stiletto boots and a lowcut black ruffled dress.

Steven heard the two women conversing, and hobbled into the foyer as Lucretia moved gracefully toward him. "Steven! What on earth happened?"

"Just a few frostbitten toes."

She lay a comforting hand against the side of his face. "Oh! You poor dear!" Steven noticed her black nail polish and recoiled, causing Lucretia to take note.

"Is there something wrong?"

"I just noticed your black nail polish. You usually have them painted red."

"How nice of you to notice such details. I simply thought the black would be a better match to the Gothic Victorian decor of this house."

Loraine moved abruptly toward Steven. "I couldn't help but admire your Dragon's Heart pendant." The two women shared an intense glare, one that brought a wickedly cold mood to the room.

"And your… radiant Oralite necklace. How befitting for a White Witch."

Loraine quickly and cleverly responded, "One such as myself can never be too careful when evil forces are lurking."

"I could not agree more, Ms. Sandstrom."

Steven moved toward Loraine, as Lucretia continued into the sitting room. "Forgive me, Steven, if I fail to contain my civility with that loathsome, arrogant woman."

"You are right to be cautious, my dear. She is quite abrasive, but there is something else about that doesn't settle quite right with me."

"I saw the way you were staring at those unflattering fingernails. What was that all about?"

Steven sighed. "Perhaps it's nothing, but Charlotte Locke also had black fingernails when I saw her in the mausoleum last night. Just seeing them again gave me the chills."

Loraine stuttered. "Steven…" she whispered. "We must talk about this later." He agreed. "Well, I guess she is here to stay for the day, so we should try to make the best of an awkward situation."

"Agreed! You know what they say: keep your friends close and your enemies closer." Loraine gasped.

Steven smiled and held out his arm for Loraine as the family began to exit the sitting room. "Shall we follow on to the dining room?"

As they entered the dining room, Penelope gestured for them to join her at the head of the table. Steven smiled; he knew deep down Lucretia made his mother very uneasy as well. Nonetheless, she stayed quiet because Daniel insisted on keeping this unbearable woman involved in their family affairs. Steven reassured her with a nod, as Daniel stood to toast the day.

"I just want to say it's been a rocky few day, but here we are coming together as a family. We have old and new members at the same table. Steven and Loraine… I am grateful you were brought to us. We are truly blessed on this Thanksgiving Day."

Penelope stood after Daniel. "Thank you for that nice toast, but I just want to say how wonderful it is to see all of my loved ones together. Steven and Loraine, we are so grateful you're with us during these stressful times."

Daniel and the rest at the table then toasted to the cook who proudly stood sentry by the kitchen door. "To our wonderful cook Martha. You have outdone yourself once again with this marvelous feast. Thank you…" They all cheered.

Chapter Eleven:

I Love that Old Clock

The group settled down and enjoyed a fine feast and good conversation before Martha emerged from the kitchen once again with desserts and more coffee. Among the selection of sweet treats was Lucretia's apple pie.

Lucretia peered across the table at Loraine. "You must have a slice of my apple pie, Loraine. It's simply good enough to die for."

"Well, thank you, but after such a large meal, I must decline. Surely you would understand how difficult it is to maintain our girlish figures."

An expression of sarcasm overtook Lucretia's face. "Indeed! Some of us have more difficulty than others." Loraine challenged her intimidating stare with one of her own. Gerard noticed the intense exchange and nudged his wife. Sharie discretely nodded.

"Everyone…" Steven broke the silence. "I have a special announcement." The group paused. "For almost seven years, Lori and I have been both partners in business, and life. I had planned on doing this at a later date, but…" He reached into his pocket. "After my experience last night, those plans have been hastened. Today, I'd like to make our partnership permanent. Loraine Sandstrom, will you marry me?"

While Steven waited for the shock to wear off, he glanced over at Lucretia, who sat awkwardly silent. The announcement suddenly gave him a pleasant calm, it seemed to put the universe back in order. "Of course, I will. Yes! Yes! Yes!"

Loraine held out her hand, as Steven pulled the box from his pocket. "Steven-" she choked back the tears.

While Steven fumbled to take the ring from its box, Loraine smiled, letting the tears of joy run down her face. "I love you, my bride to be… this is something I should have done a long time ago. I can't believe you've been patient for so long."

"Steven… I don't need a ring to know you love me. But now since I have one on my finger, I certainly won't complain." He smiled.

The room erupted with laughter, congratulating the newest Branch family members. Loraine glanced out of the corner of her eye and noticed Lucretia sitting very uncomfortably in her seat. It was obvious she had never dealt with being less than the center of attention. As the partiers reveled in the news, a swift chilling breeze swept through the dining room, disrupting the chandelier and causing all to take notice. Loraine felt the intense emotions envelop the room. She glanced at Steven; he nodded discreetly.

He announced to lighten the atmosphere, "I guess someone in this house either approves, or is very disappointed."

"Yes! That appears to be the case," Daniel III replied.

The large grandfather clock in the corner of the room chimed at four o'clock. "I just love that sound," Penelope stated.

Lucretia grew suddenly anxious. "I must apologize, but I have to leave." She abruptly stood from her seat. "Immediately."

"But Lucia," Penelope said. "You've barely touched your dessert."

The room stayed quiet, waiting for her reply as she glanced around the room. "Oh, well the time got away from me, and I do have other plans for this evening. Thank you all for your hospitality." Penelope moved to escort her to the foyer. "Oh no, Mrs. Branch! That won't be necessary; I hardly have time to say goodbye." Steven grabbed Loraine's hand as they watched her nervously hurry to leave the room.

Lucretia hurried into the foyer and snatched her cloak from the coat table. She paused after putting it on and noticed a pair of gloves lying on the table next to the front door. A wicked grin swept across her face as she snatched up the gloves and stuffed them into her pocket. After hearing the large entrance doors close, Loraine took a deep breath. Just knowing that woman was gone from the house gave her a sigh of relief.

Lucretia shuffled down the snow riddled path to her cottage where Jeff Manus waited impatiently. The moon was beginning to peek above the horizon. He could feel his hands start to shake, along with the gut-wrenching growls forcing him to convulse.

"Eww! Where have you been? Eww! The moon will rise ...eew...very soon." His breathing hardened, and Jeff could no longer control his emotions. "My ski-"

"Never mind! Here!" She held the gloves to his nose, and he sniffed at them vigorously. "I want you to lock onto that scent, find that person, and kill her. Do you understand?" Jeff shook his head wildly.

"Eww yeah! Kill! Eww!"

"Good! Now run off on your way." Jeff took a few leaps as his body transformed near the edge of the woods. "What a pity that you'll never live to see your wedding day, Ms. Sandstrom." She glanced up at the full moon and listened for the howls in the distance. *Oh, finally I will be rid of her... once and for all.* Lucretia shivered from the winter chill as she entered the warm comfort of her cottage.

Chapter Twelve:

Uncle Jack

Daniel glanced around the table and noticed all the empty plates. "It seems everyone's had their fill for one day…" He smiled. "What do you all say we retire to the living room; the football game is about to start. It's Thanksgiving Day and that means the Cowboys and Redskins are playing. We would all prefer the Patriots to be on the field, but you can't have everything." The men all stood and followed Daniel's lead until he turned with an afterthought. "Or, perhaps you'd all rather partake in a game of bowling?"

Steven chuckled. "You have a bowling alley in this house?"

"Well, it's only one lane of course, but yes. Jack had one installed in the south wing several years ago. Your father was an avid bowler."

The room went silent for a moment, while several of them soaked in the news. "Jack is your father? I knew it!" Daniel IV said.

Penelope rolled her eyes and took a deep breath. "I'm sure this subject would've come up at one time or another. But yes, Steven Spencer is Jack Branch's son."

"Wow! Then who is his mother? Uncle Jack never married."

"Daniel, that is for another time…" she frowned. "I promise when the time is appropriate, you shall be told the whole story."

"Yes, ma'am."

Penelope asked, "Would you like to bowl with the rest of the men, Daniel?"

The request voided all sorrow. "That'd be great! Can Mr. Spencer be on my team?" He winked.

"I would love to be your partner, Daniel. We might even just beat the rest of these guys."

"Yes…" Steven took his hand.

Steven turned to kiss Loraine. "I'll see you later, my dear?"

She smiled, "Yes, you will."

Audrey felt rather awkward as her husband failed to acknowledge her as he left the room.

Penelope quickly changed subjects. "Let's talk about Lori and Steven's wedding.

"Yes! I'm so excited for you two," Heather exclaimed. Penelope smiled at Loraine.

"Lori, I know we just met, but the connection between us is very strong." Loraine nodded. "We can have the wedding in the Grand Corridor, and spare no expense."

Loraine paused contemplating her response. "I appreciate the offer, Mrs. Branch. But I believe we would prefer to be married at our estate in Florida. Of course, we would expect all of you to come as our guests."

"I would certainly welcome the opportunity to warm my cold bones in the Florida sun," Audrey replied.

"This is their very special day, Penelope. You must let them make the plans," Sharie stated.

"Of course, I am sorry Lori. I didn't mean any disrespect. I just got carried away at the moment." Penelope's cell phone rang, and she quickly answered. "Yes, Lucia!" Loraine looked concerned. She listened for a moment. "She's right here! Is everything alright?" Penelope nodded. "Alright! Here she is."

Penelope handed the phone to Loraine. "Yes, Ms. Darknight! How can I help you?" Silence filled the air once again. "That's quite alright. It can wait until tomorrow." She listened, and her expression turned to surprise. "How good of you to suggest… that would be quite nice, and it would allow us to be better acquainted." Loraine looked puzzled. "I'm conversing with the ladies at present. Would you still be available in about an hour?" Audrey looked confused. "Very well! I'll see you then."

"What did she want?" Audrey asked.

"I'm quite surprised actually. It seems Ms. Darknight accidentally grabbed my gloves from the cloak table and invited me to her cottage for a glass of wine to celebrate Steven's and my engagement."

"After the poison darts you were throwing at each other all day, I'm quite surprised myself," quipped Sharie. "I'd be very cautious, Loraine."

"Why didn't she just bring the gloves back here?"

Loraine shrugged cluelessly. "She mentioned that she's already changed into her nightclothes."

"At this hour?" Audrey wondered. "I thought she was in such a desperate hurry to meet someone."

"That's right… something about all this strikes me as being very strange," Sharie replied.

Penelope waved off the skepticism. "Oh really, ladies! Perhaps Ms. Darknight decided to stay in, and she's just trying to be pleasant with Lori."

Audrey exclaimed, "The only time that woman is pleasant is when there's a man around."

"There go the dogs howling again," Heather stated. The women listened. "They sound very close, maybe you should wait until morning, or get Steven to escort you after his bowling game."

"I'll be alright… I wouldn't want to pull Steven away from his male bonding session. Besides, it's just a short distance to the cottage. I should be just fine." Audrey and Heather looked worried. "Look… I promise it will be alright, what harm could it be?"

Audrey looked at Loraine. "You said yourself, she can't be trusted. Now, you want to go meet the beast in her lair?" They all giggled.

Loraine nodded. "I promise to be careful Audrey. I will be back very soon." She patted Heather assuredly on her shoulder as she left the room and headed upstairs.

"Why don't we all head into the sitting room and have a nice fireside chat? I am sure Loraine will be fine." Penelope wanted to portray hope, even though she had her doubts.

Loraine grabbed the knob to their bedroom door; she knew Audrey had a right to be concerned. Lucretia could not be trusted, but she possessed powers equal to hers, and what was there to be worried about? She paused to listen as the dogs continued to howl outside, then put on her winter coat.

Loraine opened the top drawer of the dresser. Inside was a very precious ornament, a shiny crucifix. She gave it a kiss and placed it in her outer coat pocket for safekeeping. On the dresser top sat a small glass jar that she grasped and held for a thoughtful moment, before placing it close to her heart in the inside pocket of her coat.

The hallway was dark when Loraine exited the bedroom. She made her way down the stairs and out the kitchen exit, as she wanted to covertly leave the house. Loraine glanced up at the full moonlight glistening off the snow-covered pathway, and across the garden lawn toward Lucretia's cottage.

A sharp, cold breeze whisked across her face, sending a chill up her spine. *Ohh...* she grabbed her jacket sides and pulled them in close to her chest. At a quickened pace, she hurried across the packed snow beneath her feet. The howling dogs suddenly stopped when she exited the house. She was on high alert, sensing an eerie feeling in the evening air.

Then about halfway to the cottage, she heard a crunching noise from the woods along the south side of the estate grounds. Loraine stopped. "Is someone there?" She listened for another moment, then continued with some apprehension. *Maybe...* she thought.

A few moments later, a grotesque beast jumped into the center of the path in front of her, and she heard the guttural warning growls. Loraine paused in fear-ridden panic. The two stared at each other for several long seconds. The creature made a motion toward her, and she let out an ungodly scream. Her reaction interrupted its plan, and the beast hesitated.

"Someone please help me!" she screamed.

In the shadows from beyond the main house, Gerard and Sharie were walking home. They heard the screams, "Sharie! That sounds like Lori-" She nodded. "Honey, go back to the main house and get help." Sharie scrambled toward the house, as Gerard darted across the grounds, and onto the walking path.

Loraine knew she was in trouble and turned to realize it was too far to run back to the house. She stopped and turned with the crucifix in her hand. The creature recoiled for a moment, but it failed to force a retreat. Terrified, she reached for her backup plan. Loraine grabbed the glass bottle and started to unscrew the cap, but struggled with fear. In her fight to open the jar, she dropped the crucifix in the snow. *Ohhhh… you stupid bottle… open.* Finally, the cap flew off and she held it in front of her face; she cringed, hoping its aroma would repel the beast. In a last attempt to end Loraine's life, the beast leaped at her. Loraine side stepped, and hurled the entire contents of the bottle at its face. The creature roared in agony and ran off whimpering into the woods.

Loraine turned with intense fear and ran directly into Gerard's embrace. She struggled at first. "Lori! It's okay! The animal's gone!"

She cried hysterically, "That was no ordinary animal!"

Gerard tried to comfort her. "It was probably a bear or one of those wild dogs."

She looked at him with terror in her eyes. "No! No! It was a werewolf!"

"A werewolf!" he screeched. Loraine nodded quickly.

Their embrace was disrupted when Gerard heard Steven yelling, "Lori, are you alright?" She nodded. Gerard answered, "Yes, she is, but shook up."

"Oh, thank God…" he replied.

Daniel also arrived with his rifle just as Loraine began to regain her composure in Steven's embrace. "What in the hell were you doing out here alone at this time of night?"

"Oh, Steven! It was horrible! It was a werewolf! I threw an entire bottle of wolf's bane and holy water in its face. If not for that, it would have surely had me."

"I'm glad you're alright, but that does not answer my question."

"Steven… let's get her back to the house. We can discuss that later. It's not safe out here right now," Daniel said.

Gerard glanced back at the woods; the eerie darkness loomed over the surroundings. Then he looked down and saw the silvery object in the snow. "Is this crucifix yours?"

"Yes," she whispered. He picked it up and handed it to her. She delicately placed it back in her front pocket.

"Yes indeed! Daniel, you're right. I don't know what it was, but it didn't just go away." A lone howl then echoed throughout the woods.

Steven grabbed Loraine and pulled her in close, as the other two men followed behind. Having heard the screams and howls, Lucretia peeked through the cottage window with an evil smirk. She sauntered back to her recliner that sat in front of the fireplace. On the end table sat a large glass of red wine. The moon glistened along the edge of the glass tumbler. She heard the lone howl and whispered, *how nice to hear. Goodbye, Ms. Sandstrom.*

The large wooden front door opening, echoed throughout the house when the three men escorted the startled Loraine into the foyer. Penelope scampered into the room. "Oh… dear, I am so glad you are safe. What happened? We heard the howls and blood-curdling screams."

Steven helped Loraine to the loveseat, "It was-"

"Wait, Lori… Where is Daniel? I don't want him to hear this." Loraine greed.

"Sharie took him upstairs. He was pretty shaken by the commotion outside."

Audrey blurted out with much anxiety, "I warned her not to go out. That woman cannot be trusted!"

"It had to have been those same dogs."

Loraine trembled as she shook her head. "No…. no."

"Here Lori, this will calm your nerves and warm you up."

"Thank you, Daniel." She took down the brandy drink in one chug, flinching at the alcohol's bite.

"The hounds would never stray from the pack. This was one single beast, the size of a large man. I most certainly believe it was a werewolf." Steven cradled her closer.

"But… they are just myths, right?" inquired Gerard. "You know, like vampires and the Sasquatch?"

"No, Gerard! They've been known to exist, and I wouldn't discount the other two, either."

Daniel slugged down his brandy anxiously. "I'm beginning to believe that all things are possible in the realm of the supernatural."

Penelope stated, "Maybe we can discuss this more tomorrow? Lori has had a terrifying ordeal. She should rest."

"I agree! We'll talk more about this tomorrow."

Steven took her by the hand and escorted her upstairs for the night.

In the morning, at the break of dawn, a desperate knock echoed throughout Lucretia's cottage. She rushed to answer in her bright red plush robe.

"Jeff…" Lucretia noticed his disheveled look, with tattered, worn, bloody clothes. She hurried him inside before anyone could notice him entering. The agony on his face was quite apparent.

"What happened to your face?"

"I don't know. I think someone burned me. I can't remember."

She looked closer. "That's a terrible burn… sit down, I'll be right back." As she entered the kitchen, someone else knocked on the door. Lucretia looked around the corner, both worried and with heightened anxiety. She motioned for Jeff to follow, then pushed him into her bedroom.

"Stay right here, out of sight, and be quiet. I'll be right back!"

Once Jeff was safely out of sight, she rushed to open the door. "Steven! What a pleasant surprise! What brings you around so early in the morning?"

She welcomed him inside. "I just stopped by to pick up Lori's gloves. The ones you accidentally picked up yesterday."

"Your lovely fiancée was supposed to come over for a drink last night, but she never showed up. I certainly hope everything is alright? I waited up for quite some time."

"Lucia! Lori was attacked by a beast on the pathway last night."

"Oh, my… how terrible! Is she alright?"

"Yes! She's quite shaken, but she was able to fend off the attack."

"Well, I am so glad. You know, I wondered if something happened since I heard all the howling last night. Have they caught the beast?"

"No, they haven't. So, if you must go out after dark, be very careful."

"I most certainly will, and I am so glad that Lori is okay."

Steven said impatiently, "If you have those gloves, I need to be going."

"Yes, just a moment." she turned away to get the gloves on the end table. "Would I be able to visit Lori today? I'd be extremely interested in knowing how she fended off such an attack."

"Perhaps another day, she needs her rest." He looked down at his watch. "If you'd excuse me, Lucia, I have to go."

"Of course, I quite understand. Have a pleasant day, Steven."

Lucretia rushed to close the door behind him, just as Jeff emerged from the bedroom. "You failed me! She threw something in your face. It must've been wolf's bane and holy water."

Jeff replied, "I don't know! I can't remember anything!"

"But I don't understand it. Your clothes are saturated with dried blood. I thought for sure..."

"If it's not her blood, then whose is it?"

He peered at Lucretia for an answer. "I must have killed someone else last night. Oh, dear God! Please, forgive me!" In a rare moment, Lucretia exhibited a humane expression of concern.

"Now, now, don't get all emotional. We'll get to the bottom of this. Just be strong, okay? Can you do that for me, Jeff?" He nodded sorrowfully.

Chapter Thirteen:

Gulf Breezes

The waves crashed against the rocks below the cliffs of the Branchview Estate. Steven had arrived just in time to catch the tide receding into the ocean. He strolled along the beach, watching the morning sunrise higher over the Atlantic, its rays glistening on the icy formations on the rocks.

Steven took a deep breath; he loved the ocean scents that made him feel more comfortable. It had been wonderful to finally meet his real mother and family, but he also missed the warm Gulf breezes of his Florida home.

A nice stroll was just the thing he needed to clear his head this morning; he even took the time to skip a few rocks across the water. Although, what would the ocean be without seagulls filling the skies, lofting cries as the wind carries them along the currents? As the cold, crisp wind lapped at his face, he stood in reverence of the endless horizon of water before him.

In Steven's case, the days went by far too quickly, and the nights seemed to drag on forever. Not to mention, the limited warm days in November at Branchview. The mysterious reason for him to visit this place was quickly becoming more serious than he could ever imagine. He not only faced trying to solve the mysteries at the great house, and fighting the evil that plotted to destroy those who lived there, but he also had to piece together the unanswered questions about his own life.

On this cold, somewhat serene morning when Steven assumed his walk on the beach to be of his own volition, he would discover a new ally that was more than willing to add her mystical powers to the mix.

His attention was suddenly averted when a cold gust wisped across his face, and he heard a whisper. It echoed across the wind, in a highly seductive tone. "Steven! Steven! Come to me!"

The tone was both alarming and soothing in the same breath. "Who are you? Where are you?" He whirled around.

"I'm here!" The voice got louder.

The instantaneous appearance forced Steven to pause in awe of the beautiful creature perched on a rock. Her red hair swept over her shoulders, glinting in the shadowed sunlight. But the most alluring image was the incredible aqua green tail that matched with her fiery locks perfectly.

"Steven! I've been waiting for you."

He paused with apprehension. "Amphitrite! Is that you?" She nodded. "My father told me about you."

She drew a deep breath. "You're an amazing likeness of your father. Very handsome! If I were only a mortal woman, I might be tempted to win your favor."

Steven blushed. "Aren't you the least bit cold? I mean...you hardly have any clothes on."

"All you human men are alike. You're so aware of the flesh." She snickered. "To answer your question, I'm an immortal spirit of the sea. Cold does not affect me. However, extreme heat can destroy me."

"This blows my mind. I've read so much folklore about you, but never dreamed that your kind existed."

"So, you do have prior knowledge of me?"

"I've casually studied Greek mythology. But as the word implies, I believed it to be a myth."

"I assure you; I am no myth… There are many mysteries hidden from the human eye, and only a chosen few are granted access to them."

"I'm guessing that I am one of those chosen few?" She nodded slowly.

"It is my destiny to help mortal souls living on the land, who deserve assistance. I also comfort the souls who perished in the seas. There are many more in these waters just like me."

"Was my father one of those mortal souls?"

Amphitrite looked away in despair. "I consider his case as one of my greatest failures. The witch acted quicker than I anticipated."

Steven felt the allure and moved over to sit down next to her. "What do you mean by that?"

"Jack's flight left before I could warn him that he was in danger. Charlotte put a curse on the plane, and caused it to crash."

Steven could see the pain in her eyes. "Were you in love with my father?"

She raised an eyebrow. "There's so much more to the story, but I can't tell you now. Perhaps Jack could enlighten you with the rest. He will come to you when he is stronger."

Steven nodded in disappointment, but Amphitrite surprised him with a necklace. "Steven… you must always wear this. I promised Jack that I would give it to you. It will bring you protection from the witch."

"This witch you speak of is Charlotte Locke, correct?" He bent down as she clasped the chain around his neck.

"Yes, but I sense, however, that Charlotte now inhabits the body of another woman. I haven't yet determined who it is, but I will find out. The witch will not win this time."

"What…?" he looked confused. "How can you do all this when you're confined to the water, and you don't have legs?"

She smiled. "When the need arises, I can take human form. But during those times, you must address me by my human name, Amy."

"I understand that. Amphitrite isn't a name you commonly hear in my world."

She placed a gentle hand on his shoulder. "My senses are several times stronger than the average human and I'm able to best the powers of any witch. If you should need me, simply clutch the pendant. I will feel your energy, and find you."

"I don't know what more to say, this is a lot to process!"

Amphitrite smiled.

"Yes, I am sure… please know that I will also be channeling psychic energy to Loraine, and it will strengthen her White Magic. She must be very careful when dealing with the witch. None of you should ever underestimate her powers."

"I understand."

Amphitrite looked out over the water.

"I must leave now, Steven, but we will meet again very soon." Steven watched carefully as the mermaid goddess vanished from the rocks in front of him.

Steven turned just in time to see her marvelous tail flip above the surface of the water as she returned to her underwater kingdom. He now had a better understanding of the threats his father had warned about, and his overall reason for being here.

In Lucretia's cottage, she carefully bandaged Jeff's burnt face. "You should have been more careful. She could have killed you."

"Ouch… Be careful!" he moaned.

"Stop being a baby— Take this, and use it twice a day when you change the dressing. It should help minimize scarring. And above all, stay out of sight until this heals. You shouldn't need to explain this to anyone."

"Wow, is there a heart inside your chest? Why can't you use these powers for good instead of evil?" Lucretia laughed.

"What is it you want anyway? Are you going to hold me under this curse until all your enemies are dead?"

She turned around to hide her expression, "I don't know! I haven't decided. You may end up being more of a liability than an asset if you continue to kill innocent people."

"Then why don't you just end it? Or better yet, just kill me so I don't have to carry this guilt for the things I've done."

"Oh, Jeff dear, that would be much too easy. I can't do that just yet."

"You're insane if you think I'll continue killing for you. May God forgive me, but I'll kill myself first."

Lucretia stopped pacing at Jeff's comment. "My poor stupid friend. There is no God and not one who would ever forgive the wicked things you have done. Your soul belongs to me."

Jeff stood up, towering over her. "No God! Is that what you believe?"

"Yes, Jeff—it is reality. Don't be so naïve."

He shook his head. "You are insane."

"Insane? Maybe so, but I am keeping you alive." She smirked. "My dear Jeffrey! You just gave me a marvelous idea."

"Please don't tell me, because I am sure it involves me again."

Lucretia paced with intent. "A potion to induce insanity. I won't even have to kill Loraine Sandstrom. I'll simply drive her insane." Jeff was speechless… he had no idea what to expect.

Steven sauntered up the hill, daydreaming about his meeting with Amphitrite. He was stunned that the stories about mermaids were true, and at how she possessed an alluring quality that could entice even the most loyal man from the woman he loved. As he made his way back to the house, Loraine was sitting on the loveseat in the living room, working on her laptop. It had been weeks since she updated her memos. Of course, Bumpers rested comfortably at her feet.

"Lori, darling, what are you doing?"

Loraine jumped. "Steven… where did you go so early?"

"Oh, for a walk down at the beach. And you'll nev-" Sharie interrupted him.

"Lori, I need some help." She paused. "Oh, hi Steven. I have to choose a new color scheme for Heather's room, and would value your opinion." Loraine looked up and smiled. "Which one of these do you like the best?"

She laid out the sample on the table. "I like the one on the left. The other colors seem a bit off for a girl of her age."

Sharie sighed. "Of course! I keep forgetting she isn't a little girl anymore. Thank you so much for the help."

Steven wandered over next to Loraine and waited for Sharie to pause. "Did you get enough rest, sweetheart?"

"Yes, Steven! For the one hundredth time today, I'm doing quite well."

Sharie looked up at him with amusement. "How are you, Sharie? I trust you're a little less testy than my lovely fiancée."

"Slightly!" She smiled.

Steven looked up when there was a knock on the door. "I'll get it." He hurried out of the room.

"I suppose I should go to the study, or somewhere quiet if there is any hope of getting this done today. My publisher has been waiting for weeks."

"I apologize, Lori. I didn't realize you were working on anything important."

"No, don't be sorry… glad I could help."

Steven returned with Lucretia, who was carrying a large bottle of wine. "I hope I'm not interrupting anything. I just wanted to stop by, and have that celebratory glass of wine with Ms. Sandstrom. Would the two of you like to join us?"

"I'll have to pass, Lucia. I have some duties I need to attend to in the north wing," Sharie stated. "Have a nice visit."

Lucretia turned to Steven. "I'm sorry, Lucia. I'll have to pass as well. The contractor who's renovating our house in Florida wanted me to call him."

"Is there anything wrong, sweetheart?"

"I guess there were a few delays that might push the finish date past the first of the year," Steven replied.

Loraine reacted with great disappointment. "But we had planned so much on spending Christmas there, and even talked of a New Year's wedding."

Lucretia took note with a raised eyebrow. "Don't worry! I'll talk to him and get things straightened out."

Steven took off his coat and laid it over the loveseat. "Where on earth did you get that pendant. Steven?" Lucretia asked. It obviously, disturbed her frame of mind.

Steven paused before he reacted. "Oh, this old thing… I picked it up at the jeweler where I bought Lori's engagement ring. It was among some unclaimed jewelry that he was selling off."

Lucretia began to move closer, and Steven was taken aback. "It's very beautiful! I could swear that I'd seen it somewhere before." She remained fixated.

"Please excuse me, but I do need to make that call."

The tension in the room elevated drastically. "I do hope you'll join me. I brought a very nice Chablis from the

Branch vineyard in California." Bumpers erupted with a low growl. "I don't think that dog likes me."

Loraine smiled. "He is very particular. I usually don't drink this early in the day. It tends to make me quite drowsy, and I have so much work to get finished."

"Surely one glass wouldn't hurt."

Loraine sighed, knowing it was the only way to make her leave. "Alright! Very well!" Lucretia's mood instantly changed, as she moved across the room to grab two glasses.

Daniel III stormed into the room. "I suppose no one else read the paper today. That beast that attacked Lori on the path last night killed a homeless man in the city."

"Oh, are you serious Daniel? That is horrible!" Loraine stated.

"Ah! From our vineyard. I'll take a glass of that as well, Lucia."

The news seemed to stun Lucretia. "Do you think it was the same animal?"

"If not, then it was those wild dogs. The poor man was torn to shreds."

"Were there any witnesses?"

Daniel turned to respond, while Lucretia took the opportunity to spike Loraine's drink. "None that have come forward."

"Here you go, Loraine." She smiled. "You were very lucky to have escaped. May I ask you what sort of magic potion you used to ward off the beast?"

"Well," she replied. "I carried a simple repellent to use in case I were to have an encounter with the hounds."

Lucretia looked uneasy. "What kind of repellent?" Loraine ignored her question, as she set down the glass to organize her notes.

A few seconds later, everyone heard the front door open and slam shut. "Well! It looks like I got here just in time. I'd love to have a glass of that wine." Audrey blurted out as she entered the sitting room.

"I'm afraid there's no more glasses, darling," Daniel announced. "But let me run to the kitchen and get one for you."

"Oh please, Audrey! Go ahead and drink mine. I don't have a desire for it this early in the day."

"That's very kind of you, Lori. Thank you!" Audrey set her bags down and grabbed the glass. Lucretia stiffened in her chair while she watched her take the first sip.

Daniel noticed her expression. "Lucia! You look as though you've seen a ghost."

Lucretia reacted uneasily. "Oh! I... I just can't quit thinking about that poor man that was killed last night."

"I know! They need to do something about those dogs before someone else gets killed." Audrey took another large sip. Suddenly the room got very quiet.

"You'll all have to excuse me. I think I may have left something on the stove." Lucretia rushed to the door without any further explanation.

Loraine and Daniel shared a glance. They knew something was fishy. "What's with her?" Audrey asked. Both shrugged, but Lori felt uneasy.

Curious, Daniel moved over to the large bay window to spy on Lucretia sprinting across the snow-covered lawn. Then suddenly she stopped and took a deep breath. A smirk slowly covered her face. *This just might turn out better than I originally planned.*

"What on earth is she up to?" He pointed outside. "She's just standing out there in deep thought.

"I am glad you both noticed how she was acting. She can be rather odd at times. They do say that brilliance and insanity are only separated by a single strand of hair."

Audrey sat down on the loveseat and comfortably crossed her legs. "Yes, I noticed something as well, but I'd be the wrong person to ask, simply because I cannot stand that woman."

"Oh, Audrey! You're so judgmental. Lucia's a fine young woman."

"She's a social-climbing bitch! I'd trust her about as much I would that beast that attacked Lori." Daniel laughed off the comment and downed the remainder of his wine as the mantel clock chimed.

He grabbed the bottle from the table. "Ladies, if that is all, I am going to my study and finish off this bottle." Daniel strolled out of the room.

"That's par for the course. I think he loves his liquor more than he does me."

"You know that's not true, Audrey. Please tell me why you seem to be so unhappy lately."

She paused. "I hate living here! This place is like a tomb that you can never leave."

"It is a bit stodgy and old, but it's still a lovely house."

Audrey downed the last of her wine and leaned back. "I just wish we could have a simple house in the country, where I would be able to breathe fresh air, instead of the stale, musty smell of this old mansion."

"Does Daniel know how you feel?"

Audrey began to cry. "Yes, but he's set in his ways. He considers it a tradition and a privilege to live here among the ghosts and heartaches of the past. He'll never leave."

"Oh, sweetheart- I am sorry."

Chapter Fourteen:

The Mermaid Inn

The Mermaid Inn was a well-established restaurant with an incredible allure. It's a known fact that humans, in general, are drawn to the possibility of mermaids. Any chance to prove the myth is an insatiable act not many people can ignore. In front of the establishment was a large prominent sign displaying a painted likeness of the beautiful goddess Amphitrite. The image was so realistic down to the red hair, blue eyes, and aqua green tale that most people needed to look twice to make sure it wasn't a real picture.

The Inn was usually filled during the dinner hour. It was considered the trendy place to go in the little town of Lockeport. That evening, a patron had an unusual experience as he left the main entrance; an incredible redhead dressed in a green pantsuit entered.

"Good day." She smiled. The man gave her a respectful nod and ogled her with awe as he held the door for her.

After she entered, he stared dumbfounded at the entrance marquee that looked exactly like her.

Amy entered just as Steven and Loraine were leaving. "Steven… what a pleasant surprise." Steven recognized the voice instantly but was taken aback by her unexpected human presence. "Amy! You're the last person I expected to see."

As Steven stammered over the shock, the goddess quickly took control of the conversation. "And this must be Loraine." Amy gave a friendly nod to Loraine, "Steven and I are old friends from Brown University. He told me quite a bit about you."

Loraine stared, at a complete loss for words. "Please pardon my stare, but surely they must have used you as a model for the sign out front."

"It is quite an incredible likeness, isn't it?"

"In every detail."

"Would you two like to join me for a drink?"

Steven jolted. "Actually, we were just leaving. We both just had a delicious fish dinner."

Amy's lips pursed with amusement. "Yes! I imagine they would serve delicious fish at a place called the Mermaid Inn, wouldn't they?"

Amphitrite locked an incredible stare with Steven, one that Loraine couldn't help but notice. She reached into her purse after a few seconds and pulled out a business card. "I'll be in town for a few days. Perhaps… we could meet for lunch." The urgency in her voice seemed important.

Loraine firmly elbowed him in the ribs, prompting a stuttering response. "Only if it's alright with my fiancée."

Amy moved closer to Loraine and lowered her voice. "You don't have to worry about me. I have male friends; nonetheless, I prefer the company of women."

Loraine reacted uncomfortably. "Oh! I see! That being the case, I'm quite alright with it, then."

Amy gave her a quick blink and a nod. "Well! I guess I'll make my way to the lounge. Maybe I'll get lucky, and catch a little witch." She gave a quick wink to Steven.

Steven turned to watch as the shapely Amy sashayed toward the lounge. Loraine yanked his hand. "Incredible! What a fascinating woman."

He smiled, uncomfortable. "Yeah! She's quite a gal."

"It's such a tragedy to manhood, however, that a woman of her caliber would be a lesbian."

Steven put his arm around her and disguised his amusement. "I guess we all have our personal preferences. Mine happens to be you."

Inside the lounge area, the evening crowd had not yet arrived. Amy sauntered over to the bar and took a seat. A young bartender wearing a tight black shirt with several tattoos on his arms approached, stupefied by the incredible woman seated in front of him.

He stumbled to spit the words out: "The live music starts in about a half-hour. Whatever you want it's on the house, sweetheart."

Amy responded with an aloof attitude. "This should be easy for you, then. I'll just have water; preferably in a glass, with a non-plastic straw."

The room seemed quiet with quests wandering around, getting ready to settle in for the band. It appeared to be a cozy lounge. The bartender surprised Amy when he returned. "A glass of water for the Little Mermaid."

Amy responded with annoyance. "What prompted that remark?"

He laughed. "Don't tell me you didn't notice that the mural out front happens to look exactly like you." Their conversation was averted when another alluring beauty sauntered into the bar.

"Excuse me…" the bartender told Amy.

"What can I get you, Ms. Darknight?" he stated enthusiastically.

"Well… I'll have a dry martini."

"Darknight!" Amy blurted out to the customer now seated at her right. "What an exotic name!"

Lucretia turned with complete disinterest. "Don't you and I know each other from somewhere?"

Amy replied, "Oh… Should we? Perhaps like everyone else you think I look like the mermaid on the mural outside. Of course, it's only coincidental. I'm not from around here."

Lucretia remained unchanged by the statement. She was somehow caught in a trance by Amy's hypnotic blue eyes. As the silence continued, Lucretia glanced at her attire. "That necklace! I've seen it before."

Amy broke the stare as the bartender returned. "I'm sure you're mistaken. It's a one-of-a-kind family heirloom that was passed down to me."

"Perhaps! It's rather odd, but I did see a man earlier today with an aquamarine pendant that also caught my attention."

"With your beautiful looks, I would imagine you caught his attention as well."

Lucretia responded with a calculated glance. "I'd guess that you don't have a problem being noticed either." She sipped her martini, "I hope you don't expect to find a man in here."

Amy glanced around the room. "Being that eight men have disappeared without a trace over the past few months, I'm sure they're staying home out of fear of being the next victim."

Lucretia remarked, "What do you know about that?"

"I do read the news, Ms. Darknight. I tend to agree with the theory that a black widow serial killer is involved. I believe it might even be the works of a very malevolent witch." The comment was followed by an intent stare that even chased the bartender off.

"What did you say your name was?"

"Oh, I am sorry for not introducing myself. My name is Amy! Dr. Amy Seagraves."

Lucretia was intrigued. "Oh! A doctor! I never would've guessed."

"And what line of work are you in, Ms. Darknight?"

Lucretia straightened her posture confidently. "I'm an executive at Branch Consolidated."

"Really! I'm acquainted with a man who's a guest at the Branchview Estate. His name is Steven Spencer. He and his fiancée were just leaving here when I arrived."

"We must've unknowingly passed each other in the parking lot. I also know Steven quite well."

Amy eyed her analytically. "I noticed Steven was wearing an aquamarine pendant. Perhaps he was the man you spoke of earlier."

Lucretia grew frustrated and changed the subject. "What kind of doctor are you, and what business brings you to Lockeport?"

"I'm a psychiatrist, and I have a client on the outskirts of town."

Lucretia challenged her for more information, "Really? What's their name? I may know them."

Amy responded without breaking eye contact, "Ms. Darknight! You know I can't disclose that information. It's confidential."

"Nevertheless, however brief your visit might be," she downed her martini, "I hope it is a pleasant one, Dr. Seagraves."

Lucretia got up and placed a ten-dollar bill underneath her empty glass. "Leaving so soon? The music hasn't even started yet."

"I should probably warn you. The entertainment is not very appealing, and the company isn't much better. Goodnight, Dr. Seagraves."

"Goodnight, Ms. Darknight. I hope to see you again sometime." She nodded and walked away.

Amy watched the witch head toward the exit, pleased with the outcome of her encounter. Lucretia found herself mesmerized by the similarity of the painting as she left the Mermaid Inn. Her gaze turned to a look of seething disdain. "Amphitrite! So, you've returned as well."

Chapter Fifteen:

Silent Night

In the silence of the night, a mantel clock chimed at three am. The Branchview inhabitants were sleeping peacefully in their respective rooms, except for one woman. In the sitting room, the faint embers slowly burned out, as chilly air gradually moved into the room. Tonight, this woman would begin a terrifying journey that went down the corridors of madness. A journey that may have no offer of return.

In the elaborate master suite of the enormous north wing, Daniel and Audrey Branch slept in their bedroom, while the rest of the inhabitants of the great house slumbered as well.

Andrey found herself tossing and turning relentlessly before the dreams turned terrifying and she awoke, screaming, and flailing her arms about. Daniel was startled by the uproar, and grabbed her firmly, showing concern over her terrifying experience. She lowered her head against his chest and sobbed uncontrollably.

"Audrey! Calm down! It was just a dream!" She looked straight at him with crazed eyes and trembled with terror.

"Daniel please make them go away! They're all around me!"

"Audrey, make who go away? There's no one else in this room but us."

"Dan-" she choked out. "The demons! Ugly demons! They're taunting me!"

Audrey's screams were so loud it woke their closest family members. Steven knocked on the door to their suite. "Daniel! Is everything alright in there?"

"Steven!" Daniel shouted. "It's Audrey! Something's terribly wrong! Please come in, and help me with her!"

Steven barged into the room, followed closely by Loraine. Audrey shielded her eyes. "No! No! Please no!"

Daniel further tried to comfort Audrey. "Honey, it-"

Heather stormed into the bedroom. "Mom... what's wrong?"

"Heather, we think she might be having a seizure. Can you take your brother back to his room?" She agreed. "Loraine, do you have something in your kit that can calm her down?"

"Yes, I should have a strong herbal sedative; just a moment."

When Loraine ran to get her medicinal bag, something overtook Audrey and she suddenly began speaking in tongues. Daniel leapt out of the bed, startled by her reaction.

"What in God's name is she babbling?" he yelled.

"That is not your wife, something has taken over her body. Believe me, it does not have anything to do with God."

"Oh, Audrey! My poor, dear Audrey!"

They were surprised when Loraine came back into the room, carrying her bag and a glass of water. Audrey glared at her, begging desperately: "Water! I must have water to quench the fire!"

Loraine grabbed the capsules from the pill bottle and handed them to Audrey. Audrey snatched them like a frog grabbing a fly. In an attempt to comfort her, Loraine tried to gently stroke her hair. "Try and relax… take a few deeps breaths. The herbs will kick in soon."

Loraine was startled when Audrey burst out with a growl. As Audrey continued to shake, everyone in the room stood at a distance. "Loraine, do you know what's going on?"

"I'm not completely sure, but maybe some kind of breakdown. She has been under a lot of strain. Should we wake your mother?"

"I'd rather not. Hopefully, this seizure will pass before morning."

"Loraine, do we need to call an ambulance?" She grabbed Steven's arm and pulled him to the corner, while Daniel sat with his wife.

"Steven! This is serious, very dangerous. I don't know what exactly is happening, but we need to call Dr. Grayson."

"I agree. I'll send her a text message tonight, and see if she can get here by sometime tomorrow. However, in the meantime, I think there is someone else that can help."

Steven grabbed his aquamarine pendant; it had become clear why she gave it to him.

Audrey finally fell asleep after taking the herbs from Loraine, and Daniel laid down next to her on the bed, while Steven and Loraine went downstairs to talk. Steven set about restoking the fire, while Loraine went into the kitchen to prepare some coffee. Daniel Jr. wandered into the sitting room, unnoticed at first. Steven turned to see the trembling child in the doorway, wiping tears from his eyes.

"Well, young man… you startled me. How long have you been standing there?"

"Not long. Is my mother going to be okay?" Steven walked over and bent down to his level. "We're going to make sure we get as much help for your mom as we can, as soon as possible. I'm sure she will be just fine."

"It was Charlotte that did this to her, wasn't it?"

"If it is Charlotte, we'll do everything to stop her. I promise you."

Steven jumped when the door knocker bellowed through the house. "Shall we answer the door?" He nodded.

As Steven slowly opened the door, a heavy cold fog filled the entranceway. "Amy…" he stated. She threw off her hood and barged inside, as a foghorn bellowed in the cold night air. "Thank you for coming so quickly."

"I sensed the urgency when you summoned me. What's going on?"

"It's Audrey Branch. She's having some sort of psychotic episode. She's upstairs with her husband." Daniel Jr stood behind Steven, attentively listening.

"Are you going to help my mother?"

Amy bent down to address the child. "I'm Dr. Seagraves and yes, I'll do my very best to help her, Daniel."

"Do you know my mom?"

"No, not yet. Why?"

"Well, how do you know my name?"

"Aren't you the smart one?" She looked up at Steven. "I happen to know quite a bit about your family."

"Then how come I've never seen you before?"

"Daniel, I know you must have a lot of questions, but Dr. Seagraves can answer all of them later. Right now, she needs to see your mother."

"Okay, can I walk with you upstairs?"

"Yes, but you have to promise me you'll go straight to your room, and let the doctor do her work."

"I promise," he stated. Amy smiled and patted him on the head. Daniel took her hand and headed for the stairs. "Steven! I have a feeling I'll be here for a while. Could you please get me a glass of water?"

"Of course. Daniel can show you to the room."

"Sure, I can, right this way." He felt important.

Steven went into the kitchen for a glass of water and returned to the bedroom for a few minutes. Amy had already become acquainted with a semi-conscious Audrey. In the short few minutes, he noticed that the tension in the room had calmed just having Amy in the room. Steven left once again and returned downstairs to the sitting room where he joined Loraine on the couch. It had been a long night, and the exhaustion had taken over quickly. Loraine glanced over at him; she saw the concern in his face. She rested her head against his chest, and they both drifted off to sleep.

The mantel clock chimed at seven am, waking both Steven and Loraine. *I feel like I've only slept ten minutes…*

Loraine mentally heard Steven's statement. "I know the feeling. It's been a very difficult night."

Amy entered the sitting room with her arms folded in front of her, deep in thought. Steven and Loraine looked to her for answers. "We need to talk." The blood from Steven's face rushed away instantly, he nodded.

The three huddled together in the center of the room. "Amy, how bad is it?"

"Steven…" she paused. "Not good. She's still in a catatonic state. I have been watching her eye movements every ten minutes, and all I see are her pupils moving from side to side. It's as if she is being mentally controlled, but still conscious of what's happening. I get the impression that she might be under some sort of spell."

"Well, can't you," he looked at Loraine, "do something?" Amy shook her head.

"Steven! Dr. Seagraves is simply a psychiatrist. Surely she wouldn't be capable of doing such a thing."

Steven reacted, "Trust me… Dr. Seagraves is a lot more than what she appears."

Loraine was perplexed. "I don't think the spell was cast telepathically. I think it was induced."

"Are you saying that a potion may have been used?"

"Exactly! I think someone may have slipped it to her in a drink, or something she ate, and it worked its way into her brain."

Loraine looked horrified. "Lori! What is it? Do you know anything about this?"

"Oh my God! The drink…" She paused. Steven looked at her. "Steven, she had a drink of wine with Lucia yesterday. I declined, but it was meant for me, the potion."

"Yesterday? Why didn't you say something?"

Amy interrupted, "Steven that is not important right now."

"You're right, I'm sorry."

"Who is this Lucia?"

"We just call her Lucia. Her real name is Lucretia Darknight. She works for Branch Consolidated."

Understanding flashed across Amy's face. "I know this woman. She came into the lounge at the Mermaid Inn shortly after I saw you the other night."

Loraine looked curious as to why Lucia would be interested in Amy. As far as she knew, Lucia was only interested in men. It was obvious this woman was more than Steven had told her initially.

"My intuition was right." She turned to face them. "Lucretia Darknight is Charlotte Locke. She's the witch!"

Loraine realized her suspicions were spot on as well. She started to speak when someone knocked on the front door. "Shhh! We don't need anyone else hearing this."

"I agree…"

Loraine moved to answer the door and was shocked to see Dr. Grayson standing there. "Dr. Grayson! How in the world did you get here so quickly?"

"I left shortly after I received Steven's text. It's only a two-hour drive between here and Boston. It's so good to see you again, Lori."

Loraine gave her a firm embrace, and a kiss on the cheek.

"I've truly missed you, dear."

Steven and Amy continued to converse in a whisper as Loraine assisted Dr. Grayson with her belongings.

"Steven, I need to know more about Lucia, but can you please get me some more water? I must stay hydrated in this form."

"Sure, I will be right back."

Amy hung back while Loraine and the doctor discussed Audrey's condition.

Dr. Shelia Grayson was in her early 60s with slightly graying, shoulder-length hair. A plain, conservative woman with sharp features, and a stern expression. She surveyed her surroundings with the eye of a hawk.

"I have to say, Loraine, there are spirits in the house that don't want me here." Her statement caught Loraine off guard.

Steven came back during their conversation; he entered the room quietly so as not to disturb anyone. Dr. Grayson noticed him move past them. "Steven…" she called out.

"Dr. Grayson… it's nice to see you. I didn't expect you so soon." As she started to reply, the music box on the mantle in the sitting room started playing. She clenched her teeth. "There's a spirit in that room." She walked to the entrance doors and stood firm. "She's a curious little girl that simply wants attention." Amy looked stunned as Dr. Grayson began conversing with the spirit. "Don't worry, my dear, I am only here to help you find rest." She walked over and shut the lid to the music box, then glanced around the room. "She's gone for now."

Steven handed Amy the large glass of water, and Dr. Grayson locked an intense stare on her. "May I ask who you are, young lady?"

"Young lady," she grinned, "I do hold my age well. My name is Dr. Amy Seagraves. I'm here to help with Mrs. Branch. And who are you?"

"Dr. Grayson." She approached Amy sternly. "Before we proceed any further, I demand that you tell us your true identity."

Amy sauntered closer, challenging her staunch demeanor with an intense stare. "I applaud your perception, Dr. Grayson. When I walk on land as a woman, I'm known as Dr. Amy Seagraves."

Dr. Grayson challenged for more as she locked onto her incredible blue eyes, and Steven grew anxious about how Amy would answer.

The tension of the moment broke as Amy looked away in contemplative thought. "Do you recall reading about a red-haired goddess of the sea in mythology books?" Loraine turned quickly to listen with great attention.

"Yes! I believe her name is Amphitrite, but she only exists in legends."

Steven stepped in. "No! You're wrong about that, Dr. Grayson. She does exist, and she's standing right in front of you."

Loraine was flabbergasted by the announcement, and Amy concluded: "I am here to help defeat the witch that has plagued this family for far too long." Amy raised her water glass with a confident smirk, then took a drink of her water while never breaking eye contact with Dr. Grayson.

Chapter Sixteen:

The Decoy

The morning quickly turned to afternoon with little to no change in Audrey's condition. Amy and Dr. Grayson spent most of the morning discussing the incident. Steven finally collapsed from sheer exhaustion, while Loraine joined the women in their efforts to come up with a solution.

Penelope motivated Daniel Sr. to go outside and take advantage of the weather. She convinced him a bit of fresh air would clear his thoughts. He agreed and decided to head out to the gardens on the south side of the grounds. Once he hit the path, the warm sunshine felt good warming the side of his face, but he was so consumed by his thoughts, that he did not notice Lucretia approaching behind him.

"Good afternoon, Daniel! What a marvelous day for a walk on the grounds." He nearly jumped out of his skin. "Sorry Daniel, I didn't mean to startle you."

"Good afternoon, Lucia! I apologize. My mind was on other things."

"What's wrong? You look so worried."

"I didn't get much sleep. Audrey fell ill during the night, and we've been unable to determine the nature of her malady."

"What a pity! Perhaps you should consult a doctor."

Daniel sighed. "Steven contacted a friend, Dr. Amy Seagraves."

Lucretia looks away momentarily with a venomous expression. "I see! How fortunate that this Dr. Seagraves was so readily available."

"Yes indeed! However, though she seemed quite qualified, even she was unable to offer an explainable diagnosis."

She looked away with a smirk. "Oh! Before I forget. I wanted to ask you if Steven and Lori were planning to stay through the holidays."

Daniel looked puzzled by her lack of concern for Audrey's condition. "No. They invited the family to their

Florida estate to partake in a holiday wedding and celebration."

"How wonderful! But isn't their estate undergoing an extensive renovation? Surely it won't be ready in time?"

"I'm certain it will. He's been on the phone every day with the contractor."

She smiled and moved on to another subject. "Well, I'll be traveling to Bridgeport for the rest of the weekend, in case you might wonder where I am."

"You certainly do enjoy your small trips, don't you?"

"Let's just say that I enjoy seeing life beyond our quaint little town."

"I am sure you do." He thought back for a few moments, remembering when he was young and single.

"I have to run, but my best wishes are with Audrey."

"Thank you, Lucia! I do hope that you'll have an enjoyable time in Bridgeport." She nodded, pleased with herself.

While Daniel tried to calm his nerves by taking a walk, Dr. Grayson and the rest decided to hold a closed-door meeting. It's time to discuss the situation and hopefully solve some problems." Steven made sure the door was closed tight and no one else was within earshot. "We should be able to talk in here privately."

"Good! Thank you, Steven." Dr. Grayson continued, "We must keep this knowledge of the witch's identity confidential from the rest of the family."

"There's one thing that concerns me. I can understand that a lot of evidence points toward Lucia, but what if we're wrong?" Steven questioned.

"We have to assume that we're right for the time being. We all agree that Charlotte Locke's spirit is using a human body to carry out her work, and Dr. Grayson and I are quite certain that person is Lucretia Darknight," Amy stated.

"I must admit that my perception of that woman has been quite negative from the first time we met, but I agree with Steven. We must know beyond a shadow of a doubt," Loraine said.

Dr. Grayson concentrated for a moment. "You did mention earlier that she was a student at the Harvard Business School. I have a friend who is a professor there. I can have him gather some background information that will help in our investigation."

"The sooner we find out, the better. We have to protect the rest of the family from the same fate that poor Audrey is facing," Steven spoke up.

"In the meantime, I'll work on a potion that can counter the effects of her illness. We can only hope that her mind hasn't been too deeply afflicted."

Dr. Grayson looked upward, and to all corners of the room. "I feel a very evil presence in this room. It's a male energy that seems to be watching us."

"Yes! I've felt the very same thing from the moment we walked in," Amy replied.

"That's understandable," Steven said. "Daniel Branch II died in this room, and he wasn't among the most beloved of the family."

"I shall have to smudge and cleanse the room with burning sage," Loraine told everyone.

Dr. Grayson chimed in: "That might be wise to do throughout the house so that we don't have any sort of negative interference with our work."

A few seconds later the mantel clock chimed in the room, and Amy took alert notice. "Oh, that's my cue. I have been away from the water far too long. I must get back right away."

"Very well, Amy!" Dr. Grayson stated. "We all have our assignments until we meet again."

Amy looked at Steven. "You know what to do if I'm needed before then."

Steven nodded, and they were interrupted by a whimpering sound at the door. "I need to walk Bumpers, so I'll go ahead, and walk out with you."

The two left the room, and Dr. Grayson looked to Loraine. "You and Steven were very wise in notifying me. Charlotte Locke is a very powerful witch, and it will take a person like myself with advanced knowledge of both the occult and the powers of light to help fight this war."

"War?"

"Yes, Loraine, it is a mystical battle between good and evil. And if we lose, this family loses. It must be handled properly."

Loraine agreed. "I remember you taught me to be knowledgeable of the darkness and the light to understand my enemy."

"I taught you well, my dear." Dr. Grayson patted Loraine on the shoulder. "Allow me to go to my quarters to meditate." Loraine nodded.

The stress of the night and its outcome had Loraine exhausted, so she decided to lie down and rest before sageing the house. Because of its size, it would take quite a few hours.

In the Branchview cottage, a mysterious woman who was now believed to be Charlotte Locke stood before a full-length mirror, as heavy metal music played in the background. She was dressed in a tight black leather mini dress with sheer black stockings and bright red pumps. A favorite outfit of hers.

The mirror reflected a perfect image of the woman prepared to end the Branchview family once, and for all eternity. Lucretia completed the ensemble by fluffing out her blonde locks and reinforcing her cherry red lipstick. In a whisper, Charlotte talked to Lucia, *Oh Lucretia! You're such a tantalizing and naughty girl. You will serve me well tonight in finding another young man whose energy I will devour.*

Lucretia smiled at the beautiful image staring back at her. On the table was a box of sand; it contained cards taped together in the shape of a house. *I will not allow Steven and his little White Witch to leave Branchview. Their marriage will never take place. You know what you must do.* In seconds the smile turned malevolent. With the strike of a match, the card house was quickly devoured by flames. She looked down at the ashes smoldering in the sandbox, and an evil laugh escaped her lips.

The late afternoon sun was setting fast as Daniel Sr. returned to the house. He noticed Steven in the sitting room and joined him. "Steven! Is Audrey doing any better?"

"She took the formula that Lori prepared. It somewhat calmed her, but I can't get her to eat."

Daniel sighed. "I think maybe she should be in the hospital."

"You'll need some help. I'll ride along with you."

Dr. Grayson came downstairs. "Could I have a word with you, Steven?"

"Surely."

Steven looked back toward Daniel. "Go ahead! It will no doubt take me a while to get her ready."

Steven and Dr. Grayson tarried in the foyer and waited for Daniel to continued upstairs.

Dr. Grayson then spoke in a low, urgent tone. "I just got word from my friend at Harvard. He did a complete record check on Ms. Darknight."

Steven jolted, "And...?"

"There's no record of her ever attending there. Or, anywhere else for that matter."

Steven rolled his eyes in disbelief. "That's impossible! Perhaps she went under a different name back then."

"Perhaps! But why would anyone want to change their name to Lucretia Darknight? It sounds like a name from a horror movie."

"You must admit that it's an attention grabber, and Lucia is a woman that does crave attention."

"Yes! Dr. Seagraves did say she was a very attractive woman. I look forward to seeing her face to face."

"Is there anything else we can do without involving someone that has close ties to the Branch family?"

She shrugged. "I'll just have to keep digging until I get some answers. My intuition tells me that she's a decoy for Charlotte Locke."

"That could be. But if Charlotte only inhabits her body and she isn't Lucretia Darknight, then who in the world is she?"

"I don't know, but I'm dreading the answer to that question."

Chapter Seventeen:

Shady Characters

Lucretia Darknight, a mistress of the night, whose true identity remained a secret to many in Lockeport. As a decoy, she served to help carry out the deadly plan to destroy the Branch family, as devised by Charlotte Locke. On this night, she traveled to Bridgeport to hunt for an unsuspecting man. Since her arrival at the Branchview Estate, she had made many of these small trips to other cities and towns nearby monthly. It was the only way to feed her energy needs.

On the east side of Bridgeport was a large night club, known to be home of many shady characters. Ones that hide in daylight hours but come to life at night, and feed off the energy of the dark. The bouncers promptly nodded without question and watched with lustful eyes as Lucretia confidently sauntered through the large mahogany doors, and entered the club. A scent of her unique blend of peppermint spice lingered on the air in her wake.

The DJ worked his magic in the media booth, slapping out loud Rap tunes throughout the club's surround sound system. As Lucretia glided through the room, patrons moved to offer her plenty of leeway. Seated in the corner booth, adjacent to the DJ was a tall, well-built black man in his early twenties, with dreadlocks, and wearing solid black from head to toe. It was obvious by his attire that his financial status was higher than most in the room. He was surrounded by several attractive women and a posse of young men. Lucretia caught his eye as she passed, and he gave chase.

He grabbed hold of her arm and turned her around. "Hey, there sugar plum! What say you and I go get cozy somewhere?"

Lucretia replied with disdain, "I don't think so—"

She turned away, but Tyronde aggressively grabbed her arm again, causing many to cautiously observe. "You don't walk away from me like that, bitch! Let's try this again!"

She countered with a stern, challenging stare. "I would advise you to take your hands off me."

"What you gonna do if I don't?" he boasted.

Lucretia replied, "You're about to have a sudden shooting pain in your temples that will be excruciating. It should subside quickly, but hopefully, it will convince you to leave me alone."

Tyronde initially laughed, then doubled over in pain.

"Ahhh! Bitch! What you do to me?"

She only smirked as he stumbled back toward his seat, clutching at his temples.

Lucretia promptly turned and proceeded toward the bar as though nothing had happened. A man at the bar quickly vacated his seat for her, and she obliged.

Tyronde kept a vigilant eye on her as he waited for the pain to subside. Enraged by the event, he turned to a huge man seated next to him and vented his anger.

"I want you to find out everything you can about that bitch. Follow her to her car, and get her license. Whatever it takes!"

The young man seated next to her at the bar, Adam Smith, lifted his glass in a toasting gesture. Lucretia motioned for the bartender to get her a drink, voiced her request directly in his ear, rather than yelling over the music, and handed him her credit card.

"I don't know what just happened there. But do you know who that guy is?"

"I've never seen the man before in my life." She smirked as she eyeballed the handsome man.

Adam motioned to an open wallet on his lap, revealing an FBI badge, and Lucretia uncomfortably looked away.

"What information do you want from me?" He flipped the wallet shut and put it in his back pocket.

"None. But obviously, you're not from around here." He subtly gestured toward Tyronde, who was still glaring at her. "I believe you just made an enemy with Tyronde Simmons. He's a major drug lord in these parts."

"Really! Is that supposed to scare me?"

He subtly motioned to the curly-haired, bearded guy who had yielded his seat to Lucretia. "It should. We've had eyes on him for a while. You'd be smart to finish your drink, and I'll walk you out to your car."

Lucretia sighed. "It's just as well. I despise this loud hip hop. I much prefer heavy metal." Adam quickly gave her an amused once-over, shaking his head.

"I figured you were somewhat out of place here." She responded with a flirty glance. "Anyway, I'd rather have a handsome young agent on my arm."

She downed the last of her drink, and they left arm in arm, and the other agent followed at a safe distance.

Tyronde and his posse took note with great interest as they left.

In the sitting room at the Branchview Estate, several hundred miles away, Loraine rested comfortably in the loveseat, reading a book. When the front door opened, her attention was drawn to the discussion in the foyer.

"Are you having a nightcap, Daniel?"

"No, not tonight Steven. It's been a long day. I think maybe I'll just retire for the night."

"Please get some rest. I'll see you in the morning."

The two men parted ways, and Steven sauntered into the sitting room. "How is she? Is there any change?"

Steven shook his head. "They have her heavily sedated, and will be moving her to an extended care facility tomorrow."

"Dammit, if I only knew what Lucia put in that blasted potion."

Steven looked surprised by her language. "Quit beating yourself up, honey. Whatever Charlotte tries to throw at us next, we'll be better prepared to handle it."

"Somehow, I sense that something else has already taken place, and she's responsible. I've felt uneasy about it for most of the day." She took a deep breath and continued. "I talked to Dr. Grayson, and she informed me about the situation with Lucia. We have to find out her true identity."

"I know. Hopefully, we'll find an answer soon."

Loraine bit her lower lip. "Steven! I haven't let on to anyone, but I haven't felt well the last few mornings."

"Well, with everything that's going on here lately, I can understand that."

"I'm afraid it's more than that."

Loraine started to continue when Steven's cell phone rang. "Mrs. Porter! Why would she be calling this late?"

"Mrs. Porter!" He immediately sat forward. "Now, please just settle down. What's wrong?" He took on a very serious demeanor. "When?" He looked up, listening intently. "Please! Just try to settle yourself, Mrs. Porter. I'll book the first flight out that I can get." He nervously nodded. "Yes, I know! Just try to get rested. There's nothing more you can do, and I will see you sometime tomorrow."

He ended the call, and Loraine looked concerned. "Steven! What's wrong?"

"The roofers had some sort of accident late this afternoon, and there was a fire." He paused. "Our house was destroyed."

Loraine looked away with much anxiety and shock. "Charlotte is responsible! I just know it!"

Chapter Eighteen:

Dark Silhouettes

The Lockeport harbor lighthouse surveyed the waters surrounding the rocky cove that beckoned passing ships in the night. On one of the large rocks beneath the cliffs, a dark silhouette of a mermaid oversaw her vast Atlantic waters. At this moment, all was peaceful on the beaches below. The only sounds were the waves crashing against the rock face, along with an echo of the night birds floating along with the frigid December winds. However, that night marked a new beginning, as a dreadful storm brewed across the East Coast. Amphitrite struggled with the sinister plot enveloping her soul; she needed to devise a plan to protect those in her care. She was aware that upon the morning light, it would be necessary for her to walk on land once again. Dr. Amy Seagraves must be vigilant in her effort to discover the latest evil scheme and destroy it.

In the main house, there was an aura of sadness lurking that was pretty much affected all its inhabitants. Since the message from home explaining the horrific events at Steven and Loraine's estate, the couple kept to themselves. The night brought a somber mood throughout their bedroom. Loraine did not want to add to the stress of the situation by revealing the secret she wanted to so tell her husband. Her mind raced until, through sheer exhaustion, she finally fell asleep. Steven also stared at the ceiling for several hours before surrendering himself as well.

Shortly after one am, he was awakened once again by the sound of classical piano music echoing through the great house. He rolled over to find Loraine and Bumpers sound asleep. As he slipped on his robe, the dog lifted his head for a few seconds. "It's okay boy, go back to sleep." Bumpers obliged as Steven gently patted him on the head.

Steven grabbed the flashlight on the nightstand and headed down the stairway. The entrance foyer was dark, but just to the left of the front door was a large set of mahogany doors that led to the south wing. The music seemed to be beckoning him as he made his way through the doors. When he entered the Grand Corridor, he could see a shadow of someone playing the piano. *Oh, well here it goes...* Steven took a few more steps toward the figure, but when the dim light above the piano revealed the face, Steven nearly fainted.

"Well, it's about time you got here, Steven. As I promised, I have made my way back to the great house."

"Yes, I see you have. And I believe that was Schumann's piano concerto in A minor."

Jack applauded. "Very good! You must be a fan of classical music.

"I was trained in classical piano as a child. Obviously, it was an inherited talent."

"Among many, I'm sure."

Steven pulled up a seat next to the piano. "You know, I have so many questions, but first I need to know why Charlotte Locke is so hellbent to destroy the Branch family."

"I'll be as brief as I can because there are other more pressing issues to discuss." Jack leaned into the conversation more seriously. "Many members of the Locke and Branch families have been at odds for at least three centuries. The Branch family generally followed Christian morals, while many, but not all, of the Lockes, chose witchcraft and Pagan beliefs. My father detested the Lockes, and long plotted to break the partnership between them. The Great Depression provided an opportunity where he secretly withdrew all his investments before the crash, then purchased what remained of the Lockes' assets shortly after. It left them penniless, and destitute."

"In other words, the first Daniel Branch wasn't much of a saint himself. He must've had inside information on the impending crash."

"Exactly! In the process of serving his interests, he opened the proverbial Pandora's box, and Aaron Locke swore vengeance on him and the Branch family. Charlotte was a Grand Witch of the Dark Order and waged an evil war against us until the day she died. Somehow, she's come back to finish what she started."

Steven was flabbergasted. "That's a lot of info to digest all in one sitting."

"There's so much more to tell, but so little time. As I mentioned, other more pressing issues need our immediate attention." Jack looked serious.

"I know, and now I have to leave those issues to Lori, and everyone else to handle." Jack gave an all-knowing nod.

"I'm sorry about your house. I'm certain that Charlotte played a role in that happening. That's why you need to do exactly as I say." Steven listened attentively. "You need to reschedule for an earlier flight out of Boston tomorrow. But do not tell anyone, not even Lori. Do you understand?" Steven nodded respectfully. "Also, when you return from Florida, you and Lori must be married immediately, and without announcement. We must be sure that the union takes place before Charlotte has any opportunity to interfere. Once again, do not tell anyone. Do you promise me? I couldn't be there for you when you were a child, but I am here for you now."

"I promise… Thank you, Father."

"Very well! Now, go get some sleep. Don't worry, we will be spending a lot more time together when you return."

Steven urgently attempted to keep the conversation going. "Wait! I need to know what happened between you and my mother. Why did she ever marry your brother?"

Jack looked away with emotional anguish. "All I can say is that it was a complicated and regretful situation created by Charlotte and her father. You should ask your mother to explain it more fully."

I'll do that. But in the meantime, I also think you and my mother should talk. She's been conversing with your spirit for a very long time, and deserves to hear from you."

Jack smiled with tear-filled eyes. "I will when the time is right. I wouldn't want to startle her in any way."

The accent lights in the room turned on, and Jack's figure faded into the shadows.

"Steven!" Penelope entered the room.

"Oh…. Mother, you nearly scared me to death."

"I am sorry… who was playing the piano?"

"It was me. I couldn't sleep." He smiled as she strolled closer dressed in a decorative robe. "I apologize for waking you. I had no idea the sound carried so far in this big old house."

She smiled and sat down next to her son. "You play quite well. I almost thought it might be your father." Steven only replied with a smile. "It's so nice to hear you call me mother or mom."

"I'm glad you mentioned it. I've wanted to call you mother, but was afraid of being disrespectful to you and the rest of the family."

Penelope embraced him with tears in her eyes. "Oh, Steven! You are a member of this family, and will never be anything less. Never forget that."

At that moment, Steven was at a loss for words. From the time he was little, the one thing he always wanted to do was find his real mother, and have a relationship. However, no one could have expected it would be under such conditions. Penelope looked up at Steven filled with pride, "I love you, my son." He smiled. A sudden frigid draft filled the room, causing the light to flicker. They both turned, surprised. "Steven… someone lightly placed their hands on my shoulders." All Steven could do was smile.

"Don't look surprised. He just wants you to know he's watching. Always protecting you."

"I do wish that he would appear, there is so much to say."

"He will, Mom. It just needs to be the right time."

Penelope wiped her face. "Is there something you need to talk about?"

"I'm just worried about our housekeeper, Mrs. Porter. She took care of my parents in their later years, then she came to work for us. She has no other family, and now that our house is destroyed, she has nowhere else to go."

"Well then! You'll just have to bring her back with you. With all the extra people in this house, I'm sure she could be a great help to Martha, Sharie, and the others."

Steven sighed. "Are you sure that wouldn't be a problem?"

"For me, it would be a solution. I'd already planned on hiring extra help."

"Thank you! That means a lot."

"Now, it's late, and we should both get some rest. I'll get up and have coffee with you before you leave in the morning."

Penelope stood up but noticed Steven stayed in place. "Mother! I was just wondering…" She stood patiently, as he hesitated. "Never mind! I just want to say goodnight, and that I love you, too."

She replied with a benevolent smile, and a kiss to his cheek. "Goodnight, Steven."

Chapter Nineteen:

The Departure

Steven bid his mother goodnight with some apprehension over the impending events. The statements professed by his father were somewhat unsettling. In actuality, he had no idea what to expect from Charlotte Locke except pure evil. By the time Steven went to sleep, it was almost time for him to get up. The alarm chimed at four am.

Daniel III agreed to drive Steven to the airport, while Loraine stayed at the house in case any further complications arose.

"Steven, please be careful," Loraine told him.

"Yes, honey, don't worry. I will be fine."

"I really should be going with you."

"No, we agreed. I go alone. You need to stay here to help Dr. Grayson and Amy protect the family."

"Steven Spencer, I love you." He nodded.

Steven had never seen her react in such a manner. He started to say something, but she gestured for him to go. He grabbed his suitcase and headed down the stairs.

Daniel was waiting in the foyer. "Are you ready?" Steven nodded. "The fog is really heavy this morning. It might slow us a bit."

As they started to exit the house, Loraine came running down the stairs. "Steven! Steven! Wait!" He paused.

"Steven, we have to talk. There is something I must tell you."

"Lori, I have to go. I'll call you from the airport."

"No, Steven! I have to say this now." He curiously cocked his head in anticipation. "Steven! I'm pregnant!"

Steven staggered back inside the house, stunned by the revelation. He grabbed Lori by the shoulders. "We're going to have a baby? Our baby?"

Loraine was amused by his reaction. "Certainly no one else."

He joyfully kissed her. "Why didn't you tell me before now?"

"I tried on several occasions, but you kept putting me off."

"I'm sorry! With all the chaos, it's hard to find time to talk about anything else."

"I'm so relieved that I was finally able to tell you."

Daniel honked the horn. "I have to go, but I promise we'll talk more when I get back." He kissed her and hurried to the car with a glowing smile on his face.

Later that morning as Dr. Grayson and Amy were reading family journals in the sitting room, there was a knock on the door. Dr. Grayson assumed someone else in the house would answer, but when a series of more impatient knocks occurred, she decided to answer it herself.

"Ok, ok! I'm coming!"

As soon as Dr. Grayson opened the door, Lucretia flinched, covering her eyes. "Is there something wrong, young lady?"

"Nothing major." She continued to look downward. "It's just that symbol you're wearing around your neck. It repulses me."

"Really… Does it?"

"Yes! I do wish you'd hide it under your blouse. I'm an atheist, and I'm offended by that morbid thing."

Dr. Grayson replied in a stern, sharp manner. "It happens to be a symbol of my faith, and I'm offended that you would make such a request." Nevertheless, she tucked the cross under the neckline of her blouse. "Now, if that suits you, may I ask who you are, and what you want?"

Loraine stood near the top of the stairs watching the scene unfold, while Amy listened from the sitting room. "I'm Lucretia Darknight. I'm looking for my boss, Mr. Branch. I have some papers for him to sign."

Dr. Grayson smiled. "Of course, Mr. Branch has mentioned your name. I'm sorry, but he's left to drive Mr. Spencer to Boston to catch his flight."

Lucretia replied firmly, "Is that so? Now, may I ask who you are?"

"My name is Dr. Sheila Grayson. I'm a guest of Mr. Spencer and Ms. Sandstrom."

Lucretia was miffed. "There seems to be a parade of guests passing through these doors lately. If I didn't know any better, I'd swear they turned Branchview into a bed and breakfast."

"I can assure you that I certainly wouldn't be here if I wasn't welcome."

Loraine stayed quiet, listening to the conversation, while the click of heels on the tile floors signaled someone approaching. Lucretia appeared sheepish when she saw Penelope emerge from the open doors of the south wing. "That's right, Lucia. Dr. Grayson is a welcomed guest here, and I expect you to treat her with the utmost respect."

"Of course, Mrs. Branch! May I ask how long you've been listening?"

"Long enough to know that you have some papers for Daniel to sign. I'll take those, and give them to Mr. Le Roux when he stops by for lunch."

Lucretia handed her the files with a cowering nod. "By the way, may I ask what time Mr. Spencer's flight was scheduled to leave? I think one of our executives might be on the same plane."

Dr. Grayson fielded the question with a raised eyebrow before Penelope had the chance. "I believe he said it was a 4:20 flight to Tampa."

"Very well. I hope you ladies have a fine day." Lucretia left as Penelope watched her with stern eyes.

"Thank you for answering the door, Dr. Grayson. She smiled. "I must apologize for Lucia. She can be quite brash at times. I almost feel like I'm dealing with my late sister's personality." Loraine took a deep breath because she knew it was not far from the truth.

"Perhaps you may be more correct on that assessment than you think," Dr. Grayson replied.

Penelope seemed befuddled by her comment but stayed quiet. "If you'll excuse me, I have business to tend to in the study."

"Of course, Mrs. Branch. I hope we can talk later."

Penelope headed off to the study, nodding as she passed Loraine, who was now making her way down the stairs. Dr. Grayson met Loraine and Amy at the center of the foyer with a contented smile. "That was rather unexpected, but I think it served us quite well."

"I agree! I think we have further proof of who is carrying out Charlotte's work," Amy added.

"We most certainly do." Dr. Grayson flipped the crucifix onto the outside of her blouse and turned around to share a clever, all-knowing grin with the other two women.

Later, Penelope took the files that Lucretia had dropped off and went to the kitchen where Gerard and Sharie were seated at a small table eating lunch.

"Good afternoon, I hope you both are well." She handed the files to Gerard.

"Ms. Darknight brought these documents for Daniel to sign. Since he's out of town, would you mind taking care of it, Gerard?"

"No problem, Mrs. Branch. I'll look those over when I get back to the office."

"I also wanted to mention that Ms. Darknight was very rude to one of our guests. I do wish that you and Daniel would advise her to adjust her attitude."

Gerard rolled his eyes. "I tend to get that complaint from a lot of her co-workers as well. However, despite her character flaws, she is a very proficient employee."

Sharie scoffed at his statement. "It still doesn't change the fact that she's a pompous little jackass. I can't tolerate the presence of that woman."

Gerard tried to contain his laughter, while Penelope also struggled to remain serious. "Will Marcus and Deanna be coming home for the holidays?"

"Yes! They're coming home this weekend."

"Fabulous! I so look forward to seeing them both. It's hard to believe that Marcus will be graduating in the spring."

"I know! Time certainly does fly by fast," Gerard responded.

"It most certainly does. I'll excuse myself now, and leave you two to finish your lunch."

"I'll see you at tea time, Ms. Penelope." Penelope nodded pleasantly as she departed.

In the cottage, Lucretia imitated the flight with a cheap wooden glider in her hand. She landed the plane in a small box of sand sitting on a nearby table. She grabbed a can of lighter fluid, and doused the toy, mumbling, "What a pity that I have to destroy you, in the same way, I did your father. It would have been so nice if I could've enticed you for even one night of pleasure." Lucretia walked over to the fireplace to grab a book of matches, but when she turned around, the glider plane was gone.

In the corner of the room, a familiar figure stood, holding the plane. "I suppose you're looking for this, aren't you, Charlotte?"

Lucretia glared. "What did you just call me?"

"Oh! Come now, Lucia! I know who you are."

"And I know who you are, Dr. Seagraves."

Amy answered with a confident smirk. "Just as you did with his father, you're willing to kill Steven and many other innocent people simply because you couldn't have him for yourself?"

"Oh, like a few more dead humans really matter. I'll do whatever's necessary to get what I want." Lucretia strolled closer with folded arms. "What about you, Amphitrite? I know you're secretly in love with Steven, just as you were Jack. But you could never have either because you are incapable of offering them the same kind of love as a mortal woman. You'll always be nothing more than an immortal, aquatic freak."

She replied with much emotion. "I can never give love like a human, but I can always love with my heart. Something you have never possessed."

"Ouch! I think we both exposed a raw nerve with that exchange."

"Nevertheless, I won this round. Steven is safe on the ground in Florida as we speak. He took the 2:30 flight instead of the 4:20." She playfully tossed the glider across the room, as Lucretia erupted with anger, and growled in an unearthly voice.

"I will summon the help of my master, and all the dark powers of the Universe to destroy you, Amphitrite. You will feel my wrath."

She shot a bolt of energy at Amy that she easily deflected back, sending Lucretia forcibly against the wall, and crumpling to the floor.

"You and your dark powers are no match for me and the positive energies of the Universe that are my allies. We shall be triumphant in the end."

Amy faded from the room, as Lucretia angrily screamed with a raised fist. "Our war has begun, Amphitrite!" Amy left the cottage feeling somewhat calmed after solving the issue of Lucretia's identity. It gave her the ammunition she needed to proceed with arranging a plan.

Inside the house, Dr. Grayson urgently ushered Loraine into a study and closed the door behind them.

"What type of evidence have you found that demands this sort of secrecy, Dr. Grayson?" Loraine curiously asked.

She answered with a very intense expression. "I spent the past few days trying to find evidence that Lucretia Darknight exists, and I've come up empty. However, I did uncover something very alarming." She beckoned for Loraine to sit down, and she sat down next to her. "On a hunch, I checked the Bureau of Missing Person's webpage, and came across a young woman by the name of Kristen

Wiler, who disappeared late last summer from Pittsburgh, Pennsylvania."

Loraine looked terrified. "She had been out with her fiancée and friends after a baseball game. She went to use the ladies' room, and never returned."

"Are you saying what I think? I don't quite understand. How on earth would a young woman from Pittsburgh have any connection to what is happening at this house, or with this family?"

Dr. Grayson opened the folder. "I have evidence. Look at this picture."

Loraine's eyes widened. "Good grief! Could what we're thinking be possible?"

"It's quite evident that Lucretia Darknight is Kristen Wiler. There's only one question. Is she still alive, or is Charlotte's soul simply inhabiting the shell of her body?"

Loraine sighed. "I've known of many demonic possession cases, but never one quite like this."

"It leaves us with quite a dilemma. We must be careful not to cause any physical harm to Ms. Darknight, for we may also be inflicting harm on an innocent victim in the process."

"You're absolutely right! Kristen Wiler could unwillingly be serving as a vehicle for Charlotte to carry out her objective." Both women exchanged expressions of alarm and concern.

Later, in the cottage, Lucretia paced, nervously rehashing the events of the day when someone knocked at the door. She paused. "Who is it?"

"It's Adam Smith! I'm the FBI agent you met this past weekend in Bridgeport." She grew nervous, pursing her lips in deep thought before finally opening the door slightly, while securely hiding behind it. "Would you mind if I stepped in for a moment?"

"I am getting ready to settle in for the evening, but I suppose it would be alright."

She opened the door further, and Adam stepped in, scanning the entire room. "I took the trouble of tracking you down so I could get this back to you." He held up a credit card and handed it to her. "You left that with the bartender. I went ahead and paid for your drink."

"Thank you, Agent Smith! I appreciate that."

"You can call me Adam. I'm not on duty." Lucretia snickered. "I was very concerned that Tyronde Simmons may have tried to track you down as well. I'm still baffled by the method you used to handle him."

"Let's just say that I'm quite skilled in the methods of ESP, and it wouldn't be wise for him to pursue me."

"Wow! The FBI could use someone like you on our team."

"I'm afraid the FBI could never match the salary that I have at Branch Consolidated." Adam laughed.

"I was just wondering if perhaps we could get together sometime."

"Are you trying to ask me out, Adam?"

"I'll plead guilty, and can only hope that you'll say yes."

"I'll have to think about it."

Adam strolled back toward the door and opened it. "Well! Just don't think too hard on it. Goodnight, Lucia!"

"Goodnight, Adam!" They exchanged a long glance as he left.

Lucretia stood for a long moment, smiling while deep in thought. Suddenly, she was struck with a terrible pain in her abdomen that caused her to double over in agony, and Charlotte appeared in front of her. "This man is quite charming. I sense that you like him very much." She moved in close. "Foolish girl! Don't you realize he could cause us great trouble? We must get rid of him immediately."

"No! Please! I can take care of it without endangering anyone's life."

Charlotte leaned forward, grabbing her hair. "At times like this, you try very hard to overcome my will with your petty wants. You need to understand that you are my servant, and I can dispose of you any time I choose."

"Why can't you just let me go?"

She let go of her hair. "Because I can't. I need you to get the things I want, and if you don't cooperate, there will be dire consequences. Do you understand?" Lucretia gave a reluctant nod. "I will deal with this Agent Smith through you, and if he refuses to take no for an answer, then he will suffer my wrath." Charlotte raised her hand toward Lucretia. "Consider this your last warning, Lucretia. If you betray me again, you won't get a second chance."

Charlotte placed her hand on Lucretia's head as she continued to moan in agony. A distant laugh echoed throughout the cottage, and the apparition dissolved as her energy re-entered Lucretia's body. As the pain subsided, Lucretia regained control and the wicked enchantress overtook her persona once again.

The plane had landed in Florida with no one the wiser of the workings behind the scene, except Dr. Seagraves. Steven grabbed his suitcase and threw it on the bed; staying in a hotel still seemed surreal. Inside the lining of the luggage was a picture of Loraine. Just her image kept his mind steady. Staring at her photo reminded him of their conversation that morning. It sent joy into his soul just thinking about it.

It was quiet in the Branchview house without Steven or Audrey. Loraine decided to settle in front of the fireplace, admiring the flames dancing within. Her recent news brought a smile to her face as well. She glanced down and smiled as she placed her hand on her abdomen.

Across the room, Dr. Sheila Grayson leaned against the wall by the window, staring in deep thought at the nearly full moon, while tightly clutching the silver crucifix in the palm of her hand.

Across town in the care facility, Daniel embraced his wife's limp body. An intense wave of fear overcame his soul. *What if she never recovers? How can I survive without you, Audrey?* The idea forced him to squeeze her firmly and Audrey sat up. Daniel was stunned by her reaction. Then he realized the same distant look in her eyes. Daniel stroked her hair gently. *Shhhh, baby, I will find a way to bring you back.*

The rest of the family was lost in thought over the recent events; a blast of reality had rushed through the Branchview Estate. Outside, the moonlight revealed the lonesome trek of a black cat wandering aimlessly along the shoreline of the beach at Lighthouse Point. In the distance, a faint whisper echoed throughout the cove: "Love will lead us! Love will prevail! Love shall conquer all!"

Chapter Twenty:

A Black Cat

Across the brilliant green lawns and woods of the Branchview Estate, a black cat crept through the early morning fog. It seemed the feline was a precursor to a darkened figure emerging from the mist hovering along the forest tree line. The shrouded woman meditated silently among the ruins of the old Locke Estate near the overlook at Lighthouse Point.

Morning shone its light once again on the great estate of Branchview. But in the light, a dark evil still prevailed. The eyes of the Spirit Witch surveyed a long-neglected plot of land on the far end of the property near Lighthouse Point: the ruins of another great house that rivaled the main house, not so much in size, but definitely in grandeur. It was originally the site of the Locke mansion, which mysteriously burned down in a fire shortly before the twentieth century. Three people perished in the fire: a mother and her two children. On this dilapidated, forlorn piece of land, Charlotte Locke had vowed to rebuild her family's legacy by declaring vengeance on the Branch family. The shrouded figure turned to reveal a vacant expression; the demonic glare of Charlotte Locke.

The stress of losing their home, and the impending marital vows, brought Loraine to the beach for a long, quiet walk. Even in the cold, the ocean seemed to bring her some comfort. However, the only thing weighing heavily on her mind was Audrey. She and her allies had been unable to help her in any way. The spell was of pure evil, one that had so far kept all their attempts at bay.

A gust of wind whipped along the rocks, forcing Loraine to pull her wool scarf tighter. She found herself admiring the lighthouse, and suddenly felt the urge to walk toward the majestic piece of architecture.

The allure seemed to strengthen as she got closer to the building; however, it was not a feeling of fear, but just curiosity. Loraine made her way up the steps to the front door but hesitated before she knocked. Then before she could grab the knocker, a cheerful man opened the front door.

Bill Crawford, a vibrant, healthy-looking man in his mid-70s, answered. "Hello there, young lady."

"Hello there! My name is Loraine Sandstrom, and I'm a guest at Branchview. I hope I'm not intruding at a bad time."

"Not at all. Is there something I can help you with?"

Loraine smiled. "This may sound childish, but I've always had a fascination with lighthouses, and Daniel Branch Jr told me of the marvelous view from the beacon room. Is there a chance you could show it to me?"

"I don't see why not. Come on in Ms. Sandstrom." Bill stood aside and motioned her inside.

Loraine stepped in; the incredible beauty of the decor took her breath away. "By the way, I'm Bill Crawford. If you haven't guessed, I'm the lightkeeper in this old place."

"It's a pleasure to meet you, Mr. Crawford."

"Young Daniel comes by to see me quite often. He probably knows as much about the history of this place as I do."

"From what I've gathered, it seems that Daniel is a very bright young man."

Bill giggled. "You might say that, and with quite an active imagination, I might add. May, I take your coat?"

"Yes, thank you…" The framed artwork on the wall still had Loraine mesmerized.

"I just made a fresh pot of coffee. Would you like to join me for a cup?"

"Yes, that would be marvelous. I am from Florida and still getting used to the cold weather. The wind off the ocean was quite cold this morning."

Bill nodded in agreement. "I'd imagine that Daniel has told you all about the ghosts that haunt this place?" He took a seat across from Loraine.

"Yes, but mostly about just one. He claims to see a man dressed in old-time clothes and a fisherman's cap that often walks the beach."

"I think the coffee is done." He headed for the kitchen while continuing their conversation. "That would be Silas Burke. He was the lightkeeper around the turn of the century. Silas went into the cold waters one night to save a man whose boat had capsized in a squall. Despite being in decent physical health, he was still quite old for such a feat He ended up with pneumonia, and died three days later."

Bill poured Loraine's coffee, and she quickly took a sip. "Mmmmm, that's good." Her eyes widened. "How long have you been the lightkeeper here, Mr. Crawford?"

"Since 1993. I was a self-employed architect and decided to take this on as a spare job after my wife died. Who could turn down the offer of a free home with an ocean view?" Loraine agreed but quickly turned her attention back to the enormous collection of paintings on the walls.

"I'm quite taken by the artwork. Who was the artist?"

He chuckled. "Well! That would be me."

Loraine got up to get a closer look. "These are all very beautiful. But what can you tell me about this one in particular?" She focused on a red-haired mermaid sunning in the warm sunshine.

Bill got up and joined her in front of the picture. "I'm sure you may have heard about the legend of Amphitrite."

Loraine answered with a raised eyebrow. "I have heard people mention it quite often since I've been here."

"I am sure you have, but there is only a handful of people who have seen her in real life. However, the ones lucky enough to see her say she suns herself below the rock cliffs in Lighthouse Cove. The painting is unfortunately from my imagination."

"I must say that you did a markable job of capturing her likeness. It's quite reminiscent of the mural at the Mermaid Inn."

Bill's eyes brightened at her remark. "That mural was painted by the man that opened that establishment many years ago. He and two other men were on a fishing vessel that sank just offshore. They claimed they were spared from a watery death by a beautiful red-haired mermaid."

"Oh, my…" Bill turned. "That story just gave me the chills."

Bill was amused. "Are you ready to see the beacon room?"

"Of course! Just lead the way." She smiled.

Bill headed out of the kitchen to a narrow hallway, which led to a steel circular stairway.

Loraine stopped at the bottom. "Oh my! That's quite a climb. That must be very difficult to make daily."

"Actually, I don't go up there all that often. Everything, including the beacon, is automated. All I do is watch the weather on the computer screen downstairs. When the sea fog rolls in, I set the horn on an intermittent timer."

"I'm quite familiar with that fog horn. It woke me from a deep sleep on many occasions."

Bill giggled. "I've gotten so used to it, that I hardly even notice it anymore."

It took several minutes to climb to the top, but it was well worth the effort.

"You mentioned that the state maintains the property. I was under the impression it was still owned by the Branch family."

Bill shook his head. "It was originally built by the Locke family to guide their shipping boats into the harbor. When the Branch family took control of it during the Great

Depression, they used it to aid their rum runners, who hid the booze in the underground tunnels beneath the cliffs. After the Depression, the state of Connecticut purchased, and took control of the property."

"The history in this place is amazing. But do tell me more about the tunnels? I know they were also used as a passage for the underground railroad. Have you ever heard any other strange stories of events that took place down there?"

"Oh, how much time do you have? There are too many stories to tell in one sitting, and not enough proof of them being genuinely true. Not many people venture down there anymore. Parts of the tunnels have either collapsed or are too dangerous to travel through."

The conversation lasted to the top, and Bill opened the hatch door for Loraine. "Oh my! It is just as incredible as I imagined. You can even see the curvature of the Earth from up here." She peered into the vast expanse, imagining what it must have been like 100 years prior. Bill waited patiently while she admired the view. "Well, I have taken up too much of your time. I really should be getting back to Branchview, but I can't thank you enough for your hospitality, Mr. Crawford. This has most certainly been the highlight of my day."

"It was my pleasure, Loraine. I don't get too many visitors and none that are as pretty as you. Please come back anytime."

"I will. Maybe we can have lunch sometime."

Bill nodded. "I would love to fix you one of my specialties: Philly Cheese Steak."

"That sounds delicious. Thank you again, and take care, Bill." Bill watched Loraine as she walked down the steps, waving goodbye.

In the upstairs library of the main house, Sharie and Gerard were having a cup of hot tea, when someone rang the spirit bell near the front door. Gerard looked at his wife. "Someone's in the foyer. I'll go check it out."

He already had a notion as to the visitor's identity: his son Marcus, a well-built young man in his 20s, and his daughter Deanna, a beautiful petite girl a few years younger. Sharie heard their voices and darted downstairs. "Oh! My babies are home!"

Gerard chuckled. "I think your mother is happy to see you both." Sharie elbowed his side.

A few seconds later, Penelope entered from the south wing. "Well! Look who finally found their way back to Branchview."

"It's so good to see you again, Mrs. Branch," Marcus announced.

Penelope greeted them both with a kiss on the cheek, and she looked them over, admiring their growth. "It's hard to believe how you've both grown up so fast. It seems like only yesterday that you were both children, chasing each other up and down those stairs."

"Yes, and I could still beat Deanna to the top landing."

The group giggled. "In your dreams, mister."

"Hey, it's almost lunchtime. I'll tell Martha to set two more places at the table."

"Great Mom, I am starved."

"I'm glad to see your appetite has not changed."

"He is a growing boy, Sharie," Penelope stated in jest.

Gerard turned to his children.

"After lunch, the employees are having a Christmas party at Branch Consolidated. I'd like to take you two with me, so I can show you off."

"You certainly have reason to be proud of these two, Gerard," Penelope announced.

"Where is Heather, Mrs. Branch? I'd like to see her."

"Well, Deanna, I think both she and Daniel Jr. are studying with Mrs. Blakely. They'll be coming downstairs soon to join us for lunch."

"I think we better head to the dining room. You must be exhausted from the trip, but we certainly have a lot of catching up to do."

As the family headed for the dining room, Dr. Grayson sat at a table in the sitting room reading tarot cards. She looked up when she heard the front door open. Loraine entered the room from the foyer. "Good morning, Dr. Grayson. Where is everyone?"

"Dear, it's nearly noontime now. I'd imagine that most everyone is in the dining room preparing for lunch." Dr. Grayson turned her attention back to the cards. "Where have you been?"

"I had the most wonderful morning, visiting with Mr. Crawford, the lightkeeper."

Dr. Grayson suddenly cupped her hand over her mouth and reacted with shock. "What is it? What's wrong?"

"You must see these cards. Hurry!"

Loraine moved across the room. "Are you serious? The Knight of Swords, 4 of Swords, 10 of Swords, and a Death Card. The tarots are predicting a tragic death."

"Someone in this very household is in terrible danger. We must do everything in our power to prevent this from happening."

They both looked at each other with sullen dread. "Do you know who or have any feelings?" Dr. Grayson shook her head. Then suddenly, an unsettled feeling rushed through them both and they hurried from the room.

The LeRoux clan was gathered at the table with most of the Branch family, having a pre-lunch chat. But they were soon interrupted by the sudden entrance of Loraine and Dr. Grayson. "Everyone, listen! Someone in this house is in terrible danger. We must all stay together for the rest of the day. Do you understand?" The group looked up in surprise.

"What? Who are these people?" Marcus screeched.

"I must apologize. These are my house guests, Loraine Sandstrom and Dr. Sheila Grayson."

Gerard sternly interceded. "Ladies, this is our son and daughter, Marcus and Deanna. Now, could you please tell us what this is all about?"

Loraine reacted sheepishly. "We're sorry to alarm all of you, but as Dr. Grayson warned, the tarot cards predicted dire consequences for someone in this household. I must add that the cards are rarely wrong."

"You are kidding, aren't you?" Marcus laughed.

"Marcus! That's not polite!" Sharie said.

"Mom! That's crazy. Are you going to believe this?"

"We just got back into town, and we want to see our friends. We don't want to stay locked up in the house," Deanna added.

"We planned on going to the Mermaid Inn," Heather stated. "It's safe there. No one around Lockeport would ever harm any of us."

Dr. Grayson shook her head in frustration. "I'm just concerned for everyone, including ourselves."

Sharie chimed in. "Perhaps they're right. How can you forget those wild dogs that roam out there almost every night? Not to mention that beast that attacked Ms. Sandstrom."

"What dogs? What beast?"

"I'll fill you in on that later," Sharie stated.

Penelope lightly smacked the tabletop with the palm of her hand. "That'll be enough of this talk. Especially in front of Daniel Jr., I'm quite confident that the young people will be just as safe at the Mermaid Inn as they are here at Branchview." She glanced around the table, then sternly looked toward Loraine and Dr. Grayson. "Lunch will be served shortly. If you ladies would kindly refrain from any further alarming conversation, I should like for you to join us." Both gave a defeated, reluctant nod.

In a downtown Bodega, Tyronde Simmons, along with his 6'8" 280-pound bodyguard Lomax, are escorted by a store employee into the back office of Chaco Perez, a Hispanic male in his mid-twenties. Chaco was relaxed in his desk chair, with his feet propped up on his desk. "Tyronde Simmons! What brings you to my neck of the woods?

"I was hoping you might be able to help a fellow brother of the street."

Chaco lowered his feet and leaned forward in his seat. "You know you have to go to a higher source for those kinds of things?"

"That ain't what I need. I need some info on a hot looking blonde that lives around here. Uppity type chick that drives a BMW."

Chaco laughed. "You got the wrong guy again. I don't deal in no high-class prostitution, brother."

Tyronde became annoyed. "Listen fool! I don't need any ho! I just need to find out where I can find this bitch named Lucretia Darknight."

Lomax spoke up. "She stays on some street called Branchview Place."

Chaco got up and strolled around the desk. "You talking some rich blood there, brother. That happens to be the Branchview Estate. They own damn near everything around here."

"That so? I just got more interested." Chaco rubbed his chin, gazing curiously at Tyronde.

"What do you want with some rich broad like that anyway? She owes you money or something?"

"I'll answer questions later. Where would a lady like that hang out on a Friday night in a town like this?"

Chaco shook his head and paced as he thought. "There's a lot of little dive bars where the fishermen hang out. But you ain't gonna find a chick like that in any of those places." He paced a bit more and was struck with a sudden thought. "There is this classy fish joint that has a nice bar and lounge, where a lot of rich folks go. I got a couple of high-end customers that hang out there."

"I don't suppose you'd have a problem escorting me and Lomax there tonight?"

Chaco laughed. "Brother! We'd all stand out like a sore thumb."

Tyronde slammed his fist on the desk. "I don't give a damn 'bout that! Just want to find this bitch, Lucretia."

Chaco shrugged his shoulders. "Fine, I'll take you there. But after that, you are on your own."

Across town at the Branchview cottage, Lucretia fixed her hair in the mirror. She was distracted when someone knocked at the door. "The door's unlocked. Come in." Jeff Manus entered. "I'm glad you decided to get here before sunset."

"I want to make sure I'm locked up in the basement well before the transformation. Hopefully, you don't have someone that you want me to kill tonight."

Lucretia sighed. "Actually…" She paused. "No, but it seems like you're becoming more of a liability than an asset. Because of you, I must stay in town this weekend."

"What are you all dolled up for then? You must have someplace to go."

"As if it's any business of yours, I'm going out for dinner and a cocktail."

Jeff walked over to the bookcase and pulled the book out to open it. "Great! Just don't forget about me tomorrow morning." He entered the stairway, and the bookcase closed behind him. Lucretia smiled with amusement and continued brushing her hair.

Within the Branchview study, the recent tarot reading still had Loraine and Dr. Grayson disturbed. They were upset that Penelope took the incident so causally after all that had taken place. Loraine paced nervously, "Oh, Dr. Grayson, this is bad. Something terrible is going to happen tonight. I just know it."

"I know… it's frustrating to sit here and be so helpless."

"If there's a way that we could summon Amphitrite, perhaps there's something she could do. Her psychic powers are so much greater than ours. "

"I've thought about that, but the only way we can summon her is with the aquamarine pendant, and Steven has that with him."

Dr. Grayson paced a bit more. "Maybe," she paused, "we could go down to the beach, and call out to her?"

At that moment, the dogs howled outside, and both women paused to listen. "That would be far too dangerous. It's a full moon, and that werewolf will be out and about."

"You're right! For all we know, it could be you or me that's in danger. All we know for sure is that it's someone here at Branchview." The women looked at each other with extreme anxiety.

Loraine tried one more time to convince the young people to stay home, but to no avail, Penelope quickly stopped the attempt. As the kids headed out of the foyer, Loraine reminded them: "Please be very cautious, do not take this alert lightly. Okay?" They agreed with much aversion to her request. She and Dr. Grayson headed back to the study in complete dismay.

When Marcus, Deanna, and Heather arrived at the Mermaid Inn, Marcus let the girls out at the door and went to park the car. Heather led Deanna to a small table in the far corner, not far from the dance floor. The music was hopping, and the girls giggled, dancing in their chairs, waiting for Marcus.

Heather was facing the door and noticed Tyronde, Chaco, and Lomax saunter in and look around the room. The place was decorated to the hilt in holiday cheer. They strolled by a life-size, automated Santa Claus that greeted them with a "Ho, Ho, Ho! Merry Christmas!"

Tyronde chuckled arrogantly. "Ho! Ho! Santa Claus!" He took another glance around the room, "Doesn't look like she here. "

"It's early yet. Let's get a drink and wait," Chaco replied.

Tyronde continued to scan the room and noticed two young beautiful girls sitting alone. "Damn! Who that sweet little thing over there?

"You have a knack for choosing women out of your league. That's Heather Branch."

"You don't say?" he chuckled. Tyronde strolled over, and Chaco and Lomax followed. "Hey, there blondie! Why doncha come dance with me?"

Heather glanced up. "No thank you! I don't feel like dancing right now."

A loud thud echoed throughout the room as he slammed his fist on the tabletop. "I said I want to dance."

The sound alerted Marcus, who was getting himself a drink at the bar. "Hold on, man! We're just a bunch of friends out trying to have a good time here. We don't want any trouble."

Deanna chimed in, "Yes! Please! Just leave us alone."

Tyronde quickly turned his attention to Marcus and Deanna. "What we got here? Oreo cookies? Black on the outside, white on the inside?" He looked them up and down. "Check out the threads on cookie man, and little miss foxy. What you think, Lomax?" Deanna swallowed hard.

"Nicer than I ever have seen." The intimidation continued until a powerful force interrupted them. "Leave them alone, Tyronde!"

Tyronde noticed the familiar voice and turned to see the one woman he was looking to find. "Well! Well! Well! If it ain't little red riding hood." He scanned the skin-tight red dress, then their eyes met with intense condescending interest.

"Obviously, you're the big bad wolf, and I'm the one you came here to see. So, here I am."

Heather screeched, "Lucia! Do you know this creep?"

Tyronde aggressively got in Heather's face. "What you call me, bitch?"

Lucretia cast an intense, evil stare as she began to raise her hand. "That's enough! I'll give you guys two minutes to get the hell out of my establishment, and don't even think about coming back." The voice came from Bob Hartley, the owner, a balding man in his mid-sixties who was a tough old sailor with a salty New England accent. Tyronde stepped back when he realized a shotgun was aimed directly at this head.

Chaco nervously intervened. "It's all cool, man! We're leaving!"

Tyronde strolled by Lucretia. "You and I have some unfinished business."

Lucretia chuckled sarcastically as he passed. "I don't recall ever initiating any business with you Mr. Simmons, and I have no intention of doing so."

"We'll see 'bout that." Tyronde turned around to give her a long, sober stare before he, Lomax, and Chaco departed.

Once the three troublemakers left and things settled down, the young people blew off the incident and returned to having a good time with each other. Lucretia went on her way, and bid them adieu.

Back in the Branchview study, the mantle clock chimed ten and nearly caused Dr. Grayson to have a heart attack. "Oh!" She grabbed her temples. "My head is pounding." She grabbed her crucifix tightly. "I am very worried. I just wish…"

"I know. My heart is racing as though I was injected with a shot of adrenalin." Loraine was jolted again when someone knocked on the study door.

"Good evening ladies!" They nodded at Penelope. "I wanted to apologize for my stern behavior earlier today. I'm very protective of what my grandson hears and shouldn't hear."

"We understand that Mrs. Branch. Perhaps we reacted a bit too emotionally."

"After all, we were very concerned about everyone in this house when we received that tarot reading," Loraine replied.

Penelope sat down. "I've been thinking of that all day. What if the cards were right? I have always tended to grow anxious when there's a full moon cycle." Distant howls echoed from outside. "I do wish Heather and the LeRoux children would get home."

The women shared the tension between them when the front door knocker resonated into the study. "Perhaps that's them."

"But… why would they knock?" Loraine shrugged.

The statement caused fear to rush through her body. Penelope hurried to the door, with Dr. Grayson and Loraine close behind. When the door opened, an unexpected visitor stood in the shadows. "Lucia! What on earth...?"

"I have some very tragic news, Mrs. Branch."

Loraine's heart stopped. She knew deep down the information was devastating. "The children! Are the children alright?" Penelope demanded.

Lucretia paused. It was obvious her emotions were stirred by the incident. "There was an incident outside the Mermaid Inn tonight. Marcus LeRoux was shot."

"Oh, good Lord! Is he alright?" Penelope gasped.

"I'm sorry, Mrs. Branch. He's dead."

"What about Heather and Deanna? Where are they? Did you bring them home?"

"They were kidnapped. The police already notified Gerard and Sharie, and they should be here very soon."

Penelope went off in a panic. "Lori! You must go upstairs and wake Daniel Sr immediately."

Lucretia stopped her.

"Wait! Before you do that, I must tell you that I know who kidnapped them. He's a drug lord by the name of Tyronde Simmons. He's an insane, egotistical monster, and if we send the police after him with guns blazing, he will kill Heather and Deanna, just as he did Marcus.

"So, are we just supposed to sit here and do nothing?"

"Penelope, we may have had our differences. However, in this case, I have a plan to get the girls back safe. But we have to keep that between the three of us." The women reacted with suspicion. "He called my cell phone shortly after the abduction. Heather gave him the number. He wants me, and only me, to deliver three million dollars in a suitcase to a vacant lot down near the dock's tomorrow night. If we involve the police or anyone else, he said he would put a bullet in each of their heads."

Penelope reacted in speechless horror. "So, what type of plan do you have?" Dr. Grayson asked.

Pent-up anger swiftly covered Lucretia's face, and she turned to regain her composure before responding. "All I can say right now is that we must carry out the plan. But I guarantee that I will carry out my style of vengeance on

Mr. Simmons, and it most definitely will not be a happy ending for him." Penelope reacted with wide-eyed surprise, while Dr. Grayson and Loraine glanced at each other with raised eyebrows.

"I must go now and prepare for this meeting tomorrow. Please don't try anything. Trust me on this. His beef is with me, and I must resolve the situation."

The family members agreed to stay quiet for the meantime, but with a warning from Penelope that if Lucretia could not resolve the situation, she would handle it. The statement took Loraine and Dr. Grayson by surprise.

Along the East Coast, winters are brutal, and moisture builds in the lower structure of any building that is not insulated and maintained. In the basement of the Bodega, the floor was covered with a layer of damp mildew, making the air stagnant for anyone having to breathe it. Heather and Deanna sat terrified for their lives. The girls were bound and gagged with their faces covered, and their bodies were tied to a post in the middle of the room. Lomax had been tasked to guard the petrified girls and had orders to kill either one of them that caused trouble.

In a drier section of the room, Chaco was seated on a dingy fold-up chair, lost in thought. Tyronde arrogantly strolled by and took issue with his sullenness. "What's your problem?"

Chaco glanced up at him.

"You didn't have to cap that guy, man."

"No one disses me. The fool got in my way."

Chaco shook his head in dismay.

"Tell me! What did this Lucretia Darknight ever do to you anyway?"

"She made me look stupid in front of a lot of people I know."

Chaco laughed. "Is that all?" Tyronde exploded in anger, pulled his gun, and held it to Chaco's head.

"Anyone who does that to me has to pay a price. If you can't respect that, then I'll just have to blow your brains all over this basement. Am I clear on that?"

Chaco trembled with fear. "Loud and clear!"

He looked stressed until Tyronde put the gun back in his holster, and laughed. "What's up Chaco… you scared?"

Chapter Twenty-One:

A Maniac Strikes

A cold wind carried the mournful feel of sorrow. The inhabitants of Branchview grieved in horror over the tragic death of a young man who was very much beloved by the family. His life cut short by a ruthless sociopath who chose him as his random target. The situation was made worse when he kidnaped two young women whose lives hung in the balance as well. As the family tried to sort out the details of this mindless crime, the finger of blame pointed at Lucretia Darknight. Her reckless actions alone had led to the appearance of this vengeful maniac in the otherwise peaceful town of Lockeport.

The family elders had met to engage in a serious discussion with Lucretia. Penelope decided it was time for some answers as to what happened at the Mermaid Inn. Gerard and Daniel III were seated at the table in the carriage house dining room. "I demand to know every detail that took place last night Ms. Darknight," Gerard stated.

Penelope and Daniel III listened intently. She turned to look at Daniel. "I have told you everything I know about last night."

Gerard exploded. "Listen to me, Ms. Darknight. I want to know what your relationship is to this Tyronde Simmons character."

Lucretia sighed and turned to look back at Gerard. "A few weeks ago, I went to Bridgeport for the weekend. While I was out at a local establishment, Mr. Simmons attempted to grope me. I reacted by slapping him in the face in front of several of his peers."

"Are you telling me that he drove all the way from Bridgeport, and went through the trouble of tracking you down over that one simple incident?"

"Yes, that's exactly what I'm saying. I can't understand it myself. The man must surely be insane."

Both men stared at her sternly. "I must say that I disapprove of your personal lifestyle choices, Lucia. It doesn't bid well to a woman of your stature, and it certainly does not shine a favorable light on Branch Consolidated Enterprises."

"With all due respect, Daniel, to hell with the reputation of Branch Enterprises. I just lost my only son last night to this wild maniac, and now our daughters' lives hang in the balance."

Daniel moved to calm the conversation. "I think we need to take a step back, and let cooler heads prevail. Indeed, Gerard, this wild animal has both our daughters and the main concern needs to focus on getting them back safe and sound."

"I promise, despite your feelings toward me right now, I want them back safe as well. But he was adamant about his demands. He wants me and the money in exchange for the girls, and no one else can be involved."

"Fine, I will trust you for now. But pray tell, what does he have planned for you?"

She replied with much anxiety, "I don't know. That's just something I'll have to reluctantly handle." Sharie walked slowly into the room, dressed in a bathrobe, and her hair in shambles.

She angrily pointed her finger at Lucretia. "You! You witch! You're responsible for my baby being dead. I'll never rest until you feel the same pain I feel."

Gerard moved to restrain his wife; she collapsed in his arms, weeping uncontrollably. The tempers in the room flared as he tried to comfort Sharie. "I think you better leave now, Lucia."

Penelope sat uncomfortably in the corner chair listening intently to the conversation. The guilt of the children demanding they be allowed to leave the estate was eating her up inside. Daniel awkwardly backed away as Gerard tried to keep his wife from collapsing.

In the main house, Steven arrived back with Mrs. Porter. They were anxious to relax from their day's travel. Mrs. Porter waited for Steven to open the door, and she entered the house in awe at the sheer size.

"What a marvelous old house!" Steven smiled.

"It is, but I wonder where everyone could be." He walked back to the door and rang the spirit bell.

"Perhaps everyone decided to sleep in this morning."

Steven looked around curiously, as did Mrs. Porter. "No. Something's wrong. I can feel it. I've felt uneasy ever since we left Florida."

As he finished his statement, Loraine came hurrying down the stairs in her nightclothes and robe. "Steven! Mrs. Porter! It's so good to see you."

Steven looked suspicious. She embraced Steven with a kiss and gave Mrs. Porter a quick hug. "Congratulations, Lori! Steven told me the good news. I'm so happy for you two."

Loraine paused, trying to maintain some composure. "Oh yes! Thank you so much, Mrs. Porter!" She placed her hand on her abdomen.

The foyer clock broke the silence with ten chimes. "Why are you still in your bedclothes at this hour of the morning? Are you alright?"

His presence brought Loraine to tears. "Oh, Steven! I don't know where to begin, the last twenty-four hours have been unimaginable. We were all up for most of the night."

"Loraine you're scaring me here. What in the world happened?

"Come! I need to sit down before I collapse. Let's go into the sitting room, and I'll tell you."

Steven sat on the love seat next to Loraine, and Mrs. Porter took the chair closest to the fireplace. "It all started yesterday when Dr. Grayson was reading the tarot cards."

Loraine looked up at Mrs. Porter and saw her eyes close. "I'm already getting the chills."

"The cards foresaw a tragic death within the household."

Steven reacted in horror. "Lori! Who died?"

She choked back the tears. "Marcus…" Steven looked confused.

"Marcus?"

"Gerard and Sharie's son. Their children came home from college for the holidays and wanted to go out last night and meet some friends. We tried to warn them about the reading but they thought we were crazy, and then Penelope demanded we quiet down and let them go." She Paused. "Well, someone confronted them in the parking lot, and Marcus was shot. Then they kidnapped Heather and Deanna."

"Oh my God!"

The pain overcame Loraine, and Mrs. Porter added: "How tragic!"

"Now I know why Daniel sent a driver. Where is everyone now?"

"Daniel and Gerard are working on the ransom demands; Mrs. Branch took a sedative and is resting in her room. Daniel Jr is upstairs with Mrs. Blakely. The poor child has no idea what has taken place."

"What about poor Sharie? She must be an emotional wreck…"

"Yes! The poor dear! I would imagine she'll be incapacitated for several days." Loraine looked to Mrs. Porter. "We may have to press Mrs. Porter into service a lot sooner than expected."

"I'm ready to work, Lori. What can I do?"

"We all may need to pitch in and help the family get through this difficult time."

"Well, if you could tell me where my room is, I'll unpack and get started as soon as possible."

She stood up and waited for directions. "Very well, Mrs. Porter. You'll be staying in the first room to the right in the old servants' quarters. Just take a left down the hall outside this room, and take the second door to the left. I'll be along shortly to help you."

"Thank you, Lori! I'll see you shortly."

When Mrs. Porter left, Loraine turned to Steven. She could not contain the pain any longer. "I'm so glad," she put her hand on his face, "You made it back safely. Was our lovely home destroyed?"

"For the most part." Steven paused with a perplexed look on his face. "But something odd and miraculous took place. Our quarters and a good portion of the west wing were spared. It's as though the fire burned around it, and barely touched it. There's just a bit of water and smoke damage."

Loraine gasps, "I have to believe that it was the angels that were responsible for protecting that portion of the house." She turned to look at Steven pacing the floor.

"After seeing it, I'd have to believe that as well."

"The two of us must meet with Dr. Grayson later today. There have been many new revelations while you were away."

"Such as..."

Loraine lowered her voice. "We have definite proof that Lucretia Darknight is indeed the incarnation of Charlotte Locke."

Steven's eyes widened. "Excuse me?"

Loraine nodded. "Oh, yes, it is true."

In the basement of Lucretia's lair, Jeff Manus was resting uncomfortably against the wall. His legs were shackled to a long chain. The noise of someone coming down the stairs startled him awake. "It took you long enough. I was beginning to think you had forgotten about me."

Lucretia snickered as she took the key out of her pocket to unlock the shackle. "Don't even start with me. You wouldn't believe the misery I've endured since I saw you last evening."

Jeff yelped when she pulled his leg from the metal clamp. "You think my night's been any better?"

"Your ankle is swollen. You must have tried very hard to pull yourself free."

"Ya, think?" he replied.

"Don't be coy with me. Come on, get up."

Lucretia grabbed his arm. Jeff struggled to stand. "Oww! It hurts like hell!"

Lucretia tried to steady him. "Let me help you up the stairs, and we'll put some ice on it."

"You're all heart, Lucia!"

"Just hold on to me… don't be a baby." She smirked.

Lucretia helped him through the open bookcase and to a cushioned chair. "Here! Rest your leg on this ottoman."

"I can't endure another night in that basement."

"You won't have to. I have other plans."

Jeff chuckled. "I suppose you found another person for me to kill," Lucretia spoke as she walked to the kitchen. "Actually, after much thought, I've decided it would benefit both of us if I lifted the curse on you after tonight."

"Tomorrow? Why not right now?"

She returned with an icepack. "I have my reasons. Here, this should help with the swelling."

She placed the pack firmly on his ankle. "You never did explain the reason for inflicting me with this curse, other than it was payback for something my great grandfather did. What was that all about?"

Lucretia sat down next to him. "Your great grandfather was a crooked banker that helped Daniel Branch the first purchase all my family's assets when the value was low. They robbed my ancestors of every penny they had."

"I'm sorry, Lucia! I never knew."

"As his only surviving ancestor, you had to pay the price for his sins; just as the entire Branch family will have to pay for theirs." Lucretia got up and put on her coat. "You can stay here for the rest of the day. I have a lot to take care of, but I will be back later this afternoon."

Jeff grabbed her by the coat sleeve. "Wait! I must ask you something. Before I transformed last night, I saw a glow and heard what sounded like distant screams coming from behind that closed door in the basement. What's in that room?"

Lucretia's expression turned evil. "That's no concern of yours. You're to never go into that room, and you should never ask about it ever again. Do you understand?" Jeff nodded timidly. "If you get hungry, there's plenty of food in the kitchen."

Jeff found Lucretia's change in behavior alarming, but at this point, he would tolerate anything to get out of this mess and get his life back. As she continued to glare at him, he leaned back in the chair while the ice numbed his ankle. "Where exactly are you going?" he asked.

"Well, that's none of your business. Just don't leave this house. Do you hear me?"

"Yes, ma'am." A sudden chill drifted through the room.

Across the estate in the Grand Corridor, Dr. Grayson strolled through the great room, admiring the large antique chandelier. She was completely amazed by the detail in the architecture, but her admiration was suddenly interrupted when a presence entered the room. "Well, hello there." Maggie waved shyly. "I bet you're the little girl that's been watching me since I got here. Am I right?"

She nodded. "My name is Maggie. What's yours?"

"My name is Dr. Sheila Grayson."

"Are you a real doctor?"

The question caught her off guard. "I'm a professor of parapsychology. Do you know what that is?" She shook her head no. "Think of me as an expert on the supernatural, such as beings like yourself."

"Are you here to send us back?"

"On the contrary. I want to find out why you're here."

Maggie looked up with innocent eyes. "We all came back to help."

Dr. Grayson was perplexed. "You keep saying we. Who else is here?"

"All the good members of the Branch family. My older brother Andrew and his fiancée Beth are on their way. He'll protect me from my mean brother Daniel."

Dr. Grayson looked interested. "Why are you so scared of your brother Daniel?"

"He hurt me." Maggie glanced around the room and changed the subject.

"Someone died, didn't they?"

Maggie nodded sadly. "I died in this room a long, long time ago."

"What happened, Maggie?"

"Daniel killed me. He was jealous of me." Maggie pointed to the center of the room. "There was a large statue that used to be there. Daniel was chasing me, and I hid behind it. He pushed it over on me, and said it was an accident."

"I'm so sorry that happened to you, Maggie."

Maggie grew increasingly anxious. "I have to go now. Daniel's coming." She then vanished. Dr. Grayson was left in awe at her experience but disturbed by Maggie's declaration. Her suspicions were accurate.

The rest of the day went off without a hitch. All seemed quiet on the home front for the meantime. Most of the inhabitants of the great house remained in their respective places meditating on the recent turn of events, wondering what else would befall the family in the near future.

Daniel ordered Lucretia to meet him at his office that afternoon to review the upcoming plan to get the girls home safely. In a pleasant twist, Lucretia seemed unusually helpful. "Tell me again how this is going to play out."

She replied with a slight notion of disdain for the continued barrage of questions. "Okay! I'll meet Tyronde in the abandoned parking lot at five o'clock. The sun will be down, and the full moon won't appear on the horizon until nearly six o'clock. So, it should be quite dark, as he wanted it. We'll exchange the money, and I'll give the girls my keys and tell them to drive straight to Branchview."

Daniel reacted with much anxiety. "What about you, Lucia? What will this crazy beast of a man do to you? We simply have to tell the police about the meeting."

"Absolutely not, Daniel! He's as smart as he is insane. We must play this thing right, or Tyronde will kill all three of us."

Daniel got up and paced nervously. "So, we're letting him walk away with you, and three million dollars of our money."

Lucretia got up and paced as well. "The police know who he is. He won't get far. Besides, I never mentioned this before, but on the night, I had my first encounter with Tyronde, I was approached by an undercover FBI agent named Adam Smith."

Daniel paused to listen with great interest. "He's had Tyronde under surveillance for several months now. I have his card, so I'll notify him ahead of time, and tell him the situation. No matter where he tries to hide, I'm certain that agent Smith will know how to find him." Daniel gave a nervous nod of agreement.

The whole scene left Daniel very uncomfortable, but under the circumstances, he had no choice other than to trust Lucretia. It was a matter of life or death with the girls. While Daniel tried to keep busy with work, securing the money, Steven decided to visit Gerard and Sharie to give his condolences.

He spent his walk there trying to uncover the best way to expel his sorrow and not make a horrible matter worse. As Steven climbed the stairs, the door seemed to get farther away. He dreaded the reason for his visit, and could only imagine how he might feel if the tables were turned.

Gerard reached for the doorknob to open the door. "Steven! When did you get back?"

"I arrived early this morning and wanted to stop by and offer my condolences. Is there anything I can do to help?"

"I appreciate your concern, but there's not much any of us can do right now but wait."

Sharie entered from the living room. "I think we should share our thoughts about Ms. Darknight with Mr. Spencer."

"Sharie! Now's not an appropriate time."

Sharie moved closer. "I think it's a perfect time. I'm sure Steven would agree that it's more than a coincidence that all the problems at Branchview started right about the time that Lucretia arrived here." She stood in front of Steven. "We also find it interesting that she was somewhat indirectly involved in all the unfortunate circumstances that have taken place." She moved over next to Steven. "We always thought it was rather odd that she wanted to rent that cottage as well. The place had been boarded up and vacant for nearly forty years. Ever since the death of Charlotte Locke."

Steven's interest was suddenly piqued. "Charlotte Locke? What can you tell me about that?"

"I was just a child, but I can remember them carrying her charred body from the cottage."

"Was there a fire?"

"Only in the basement. They claimed it was a tragic accident, but I remember the adults whispering something about Daniel Branch the Second being responsible."

Steven looked perplexed. "I don't quite understand. Why would he want to kill his sister in law?"

"Because Charlotte was a witch, and she brought the same misery to Branchview that we're experiencing now."

Gerard reluctantly joined in. "We also believe there's something strange going on in the tunnels below the cottage. One of the closed-off tunnels leads to the garage beneath our house. Sometimes at night, we hear agonizing screams and voices echoing from somewhere behind the boarded-up entrance."

Sharie replied, "Just before your arrival, one of our groundskeepers discovered something down there. Before he could tell anyone, he was tragically killed."

"Was that Mr. McAndrew?" Both nodded.

Gerard answered, "We believe that Lucia might be a witch. Possibly from the same coven as Charlotte, and that somewhere in those tunnels is a passageway that leads directly to hell."

Steven's eyes widened as the conversation paused. "You both have to promise me that you will not mention it to any other person." Gerard and Sharie shared a glance. "Lori, Dr. Grayson, and I all agree that Lucia is indeed a witch. But we also think that she is the incarnation of Charlotte Locke."

Sharie looked at Gerard. "Are you saying that Charlotte Locke has returned from the dead?"

Steven gave a definite nod. "And she's using the body of Lucia Darknight, or whoever that poor unfortunate woman may be."

"Good Lord! How could this be happening?"

Sharie stood up and paced in a fit of emotion. "How can we stop her? She'll destroy all of us."

Steven held the aquamarine pendant between his fingers. "I'll arrange a meeting where we can discuss everything. But no matter what, we will find a way."

The tensions on the Branchview home front continued to build as the moment of truth got closer. It all came down to trusting the last person anyone could have ever expected, Lucretia Darknight, or most likely Charlotte Locke. But at this point, the only way Daniel and Gerard would get their children home safely was to let Lucretia complete her plan.

Inside a large empty warehouse, Tyronde, Lomax, and Chaco were shoving the blindfolded and gagged girls into a dark corner of the building. As they paced around the enormous room, Tyronde screamed, "Lomax, go check the rest of the building to make sure there ain't no hidden surprises."

"Why me? Send Chaco…"

"I said you. Now go before I shoot you like I did that stupid kid."

Deanna tried to hold back her fear, but muffled sobs drifted through the air. "What did you say, bitch? You better just shut up."

Heather grabbed Deanna's arm to help keep her calm. She knew Tyronde was unstable and anything little might set him off again.

Lomax returned. "It's all clear boss."

"Good!" He looked around at the high ceiling with windows surrounding the peak. "That bitch Lucretia is one smart lady. Ain't nobody gonna see nothing in here like they would in that parking lot."

"What if it's a trap?"

Tyronde laughed, "Anybody tries to take us down; these bitches are going down permanent. You dig?" The girls pleaded through their gags.

A car pulled up outside. "Lomax, go see who that is—"

Before he could peek outside, Lucretia casually strolled in, toting a suitcase, and breezed by him.

"Good evening, gentlemen!" Lucretia halted at a safe distance.

"I see you brought my money. Let's get down to business."

"First, you need to let the girls go—"

"No! First…" he motioned with his gun, "you need to show me the money."

Lucretia sighed. "Fine." She opened the zipper revealing the large stacks of bills.

Tyronde let loose with a sinister laugh "You can zip that back up now." Chaco and Lomax broke into wide evil grins. "Good, now hand it over." He turned and nodded to Lomax, who took the blindfolds and gags off of the girls, untied them, and pushed them forward.

The girls hurried to Lucretia, and she whispered as she handed Heather the car keys. "Take my car, drive back to Branchview, and don't tell anyone that you were ever in this place. Do you understand?" They nodded. "Now hurry!"

"What about you, Lucia?" Heather blurted out.

"Don't worry about me. Just make sure you tell everyone that you were let go in a parking lot. Do you understand?" They both nodded with perplexed expressions and hurried from the warehouse.

Tyronde then arrogantly strolled toward Lucretia, coming within inches of her face. "Well, well! I've waited a long time for this."

"Just what do you want from me?"

He chuckled. "I want to know what kind of voodoo magic you worked on me that night. Got a feeling that info might be worth more than that three million you got there."

"There was no magic. I simply bruised that enormous ego of yours by refusing your chauvinistic advances."

Tyronde angrily slapped her across the face. "You can't talk to me that way, bitch. Now, this is what we gonna do. We gonna walk out of here with my money and go to a nice cozy place where I can get to know that sexy little body of yours. Then, you gonna tell me everything I need to know about this magic power you have."

"Then what?"

"That's for me to know, and for you to find out."

Lucretia gave a disparaging motion. "Very well! But first, we need to get something out of the way."

Lucretia swiftly waved her hand toward them, and all three men were propelled against a wall, where they were unable to move against the invisible force that held them there. Chaco screamed like a girl, "What the hell! I can't move."

Lucretia strolled over and surveyed all three struggling men with an evil grin. "Man! She got some kinda weird power!" Lomax exclaimed.

"Tyronde, you should have left well enough alone."

"Who the hell are you?"

Lucretia stepped closer and ran her long red fingernail up his throat to his chin. "I'm your worst nightmare, bitch!" Lucretia turned and sashayed away from them.

"Where are you going? I'll get outta here and kill ya. I promise."

Lucretia halted by the suitcase. "Don't make promises you can't keep, Mr. Simmons. I hate to leave you gentlemen hanging, but I must leave now with my three million dollars."

Through the darkened room, echoes of Lucretia's heels tapped against the concrete floor. As she approached the doorway, the moon's reflection illuminated through the skylight. Lucretia let loose with a wicked laugh that echoed throughout the empty warehouse. She turned toward a large sliding steel door that connected to another portion of the warehouse. A smooth motion of her hand brought forth a creaking sound, as the bulky door slowly slid open.

Jeff stumbled from the room, amid his transformation. He doubled over in pain, and when he stood erect, the beast roared as it spotted the three men trapped against the wall. They shrieked in fear. "What the hell is that thing?"

"Man! This can't be real!"

"No! No! Don't leave us here with that freak!"

Lucretia clutched the large pentagram around her neck as the werewolf charged at the three men, and they screamed in terror. Her evil laugh reverberated over the growls and gnashes. Then she pulled a long, thick chain through the handle and padlocked the door, as horrible growls and screams reverberated from inside.

As she headed across the parking lot, she placed a call on her cell phone. "Yes! Mr. Augustine? This is Ms. Darknight from Branch Consolidated. I hate to bother you on a Sunday evening, but I'm calling about that warehouse on Water Street that is scheduled to be demolished next week." She paused to listen. "Yes! Is there a chance that you could schedule that sooner? We have plans that we'd like to move forward with for that property." She listened, then smiled to herself. "The day after Christmas? That would be excellent, Mr. Augustine. I cannot thank you enough."

The conversation paused. "Yes! Have a pleasant evening, and a very happy holiday as well." Lucretia ended the call and glanced up at the full moon. "Farewell, Mr. Simmons. That was the hardest but most rewarding three million dollars that I could ever earn." She buttoned her coat, turned her collar up, and slowly strolled away, down the cold, empty street, dragging the suitcase.

Chapter Twenty-Two:

The Arrival

The horrific scene fell silent as a light dusting of snow fell on the ground around the warehouse district of Lockeport. It is amazing how the dawn of a new day can bring about enlightenment. The adage could be, those who live violently, die in the same manner. As the sun rose, one young man woke in an abandoned warehouse, to witness a horrible reality. The cursed beast he had transformed into the previous night was responsible for bringing such a fate to three ruthless, vicious men.

A pickup truck pulled up and parked in front of the warehouse, and Lucretia Darknight emerged from the vehicle. Jeff Manus lay on the cold cement floor wearing tattered, bloody clothing. He jumped to his feet when he heard the door open, the morning light revealed a silhouette of Lucretia. She walked over and dropped a gym bag on the ground next to him. "I brought you a change of clothes."

"It's about time you got here."

Lucretia looked around, shivering at the sight. Jeff took notice, "My thoughts exactly. Who were these poor unfortunate souls? Was I responsible for all this?"

"Yes, I am afraid so, but they were far from innocent. They were very evil men who deserved every bit of their fate."

"They'd have to be pretty bad to be eviler than you."

"Really, Jeffrey! I did come back for you as I promised, didn't I?" Jeff sighed. "Before you change into those fresh clothes, I need you to do one more thing." He gave her a stern stare. "I'll need you to drag their remains down to the sub-basement."

"Good God!" he shrieked. "You expect me to touch those mutilated corpses?"

"We don't have a choice; their bodies can never be found."

Jeff displayed a reluctant agreement, "After I do that, then what?"

"Then, as I promised, I will free you forever from your curse, and in return, you will deny ever having any involvement with me." He wholeheartedly agreed.

In the dining room at Branchview, the mood had elevated somewhat with the girls home safely. Other than being exhausted, they were in good health. Daniel Sr. brought Agent Smith in to talk with the girls, and they greeted him with empty, sober expressions. He addressed Heather first: "I know you two have been asked a million questions already this morning, but hopefully you can give me some clues as to where they may have taken Ms. Darknight."

"We have no idea. We were blindfolded for most of the time, so we don't know where they were keeping us."

"So basically, the only time they ever removed the blinders was when they let you go in the parking lot. Is that correct?" Both girls cautiously glanced at each other and nodded.

Both Adam and Daniel noticed the girls' hesitant reaction. "Are you certain you two are telling us everything?"

Deanna blurted out, "Yes! All we know is that Ms. Darknight handed us her car keys, and that's the last time we saw her."

Daniel Sr replied, "With all due respect Agent Smith, didn't Lucia call and inform you of her plans ahead of time?"

Adam shook his head. "I didn't know anything about all this until after it happened."

Daniel looked puzzled. "That's odd. She assured me you were notified."

"Perhaps she was scared, and changed her mind?" Daniel remained quiet. He did not want to stir up more questions than he wanted to answer.

Penelope rushed into the dining room. "They've found Lucia!"

"Where? Is she still alive?"

Penelope paused to breathe, "She's at a truck stop on the interstate, somewhere between here and Boston. Detective Fuller just received word, and she's on her way back to Lockeport as we speak."

"Did they apprehend that scoundrel Simmons as well?"

"No, I guess not. They dumped her off on the side of the road and left her there."

Adam pursed his lips while deep in thought. "There's something strange about all of this. That doesn't sound like something Tyronde would do. I'd better catch up with Fuller and find out all the details."

"Come, Agent Smith, I'll walk out with you."

The girls waited impatiently until the detective left the room. "Now that I know Ms. Darknight is safe, I think I'll go lie down and take a nap."

Penelope patted Deanna on the shoulder as she walked past. "Oh, Heather! When will this nightmare ever end?" Heather broke down in tears, Penelope quickly comforted her with a hug.

"Oh, Gramma! I must tell you… no one else knew, but Marcus and I had been secretly dating since last summer."

Penelope continues to hug her. "Oh, sweetheart! I am so sorry."

"We'd planned on telling everyone tonight on Christmas Eve." The calmness in her voice turned to uncontrollable sobbing. "Honey, I don't know what to say, but believe me, life moves on and you will learn to live with this. I promise."

Heather looked at her with questions in her eyes. "I'm not sure about that Gramma…"

"I know you will. Just as I learned…" she sobbed.

Days later, after Marcus's funeral, Steven, Loraine, Dr. Grayson, and Sharie waited in the sitting room for the rest of the family to return. All were silent until the mantel clock chimed at 5 pm. It nearly scared Loraine to death. "Oh," she blurted out. Steven grabbed her shoulders and pulled her in close.

Their dark attire matched the mood shared among all of the family members. Steven held Loraine while Dr. Grayson stared out the window. They all tried to comfort Sharie, but nothing short of time was going to take away her pain.

"Sharie…" Loraine announced, "Marcus must've been an extremely amicable young man. I believe most of the population of Lockeport showed up for his viewing."

"He was a good boy. He didn't deserve to die the way he did." She looked upward for a moment. "I hope he understands that I couldn't be there when they closed his casket."

"I'm sure that he knows how hurt you are, Sharie. You needn't feel guilty."

"Could I get you a brandy?" Loraine asked.

"Actually, yes. Thank you so much, Lori… You know, I would have never dreamed that I'd be mourning my son's death on Christmas Eve. It's supposed to be a happy time of the year."

As Lori got up to pour the drink, Steven spoke up: "You're right, Sharie. We should mourn his death this evening as planned, but I also think we need to celebrate life at the same time."

He continued while Loraine handed the drink to Sharie. "The night before I left for Florida, my father appeared to me in the Grand Corridor and made it very clear that Lori and I needed to get married as soon as possible. The next morning, I found out that we were having a baby." He paused to smile admirably at Loraine, then looked toward Sharie. "I'm not wasting any more time. I'd like to ask, that along with the wake, we can also celebrate our wedding tonight."

"But Steven, where could we possibly find a minister on such short notice, and on Christmas Eve no less?" Loraine questioned.

"Well… Loraine," Dr. Grayson spoke up, "I'm certified by the state of Connecticut. I can perform the ceremony."

A slight breeze whistled through the room, raising the sheer curtains on the window and causing everyone to take notice. The lights also flickered, and the music box on the mantle began playing of its own accord. Steven stood up to close the lid, and as he turned Dr. Grayson had a slight smile. "I do believe that our little ghost, Maggie, is showing her approval."

"Do we have your blessing as well, Sharie?"

Sharie raised her drink toward Steven in a toast. "Yes, you do. So, it shall be."

They exchanged a grateful nod. "We all have much to do beforehand. Lori, I'll need you and Dr. Grayson to clear the house of any negative energies and I'll place a crucifix at all the entrance doors."

"Good idea! That should keep the witch away." Sharie announced.

"Sharie, you can tell the others what we have planned when they return from the funeral home. We will not let the forces of evil continue to tear this family apart." Steven paused in thought and clutched the aquamarine pendant tightly in his hand as the women got up, and moved into action. "On this night, only light will fill the house of Branchview."

The family was determined to turn what was left of a miserable Christmas into something positive. However, across town at Branch Consolidated Headquarters, Lucretia had set her recent experience behind her and was moving forward with her plans. The phone rang as she waited in her office, and she casually answered it. "Yes, Marvin! Key them into the elevator, and send them right up."

Lucretia hung up the phone and reached into her clutch purse for a compact mirror. Inside was a powder pad to dab her nose, and she then took a moment to touch up her brilliant lipstick. She heard someone clearing their throat in the hallway, it echoed off the walls. A man in his mid-sixties with slight graying on the sides of his jet-black hair entered the office. His attire spoke volumes as to his stature. Lucretia graciously moved to the entrance and met her highly affluent guest, Senator Richard Holdsclaw. He was followed by Representative Linda Lapino. She was in her early 70s. An impeccably dressed woman with perfectly coiffed hair.

"Ms. Darknight! Thank you so much for meeting with us at this hour."

"It's not like I have anything better to do on Christmas Eve."

They both sat across the conference table. "We quite understand, we don't celebrate either. As a matter of fact, we intend to one day abolish the holiday altogether."

"What a noble achievement that will be."

She sarcastically glanced toward Representative Lapino. "By the way, I love your dress."

Lapino shrugged off the compliment with a haughty smile. "I can sense that you're not quite enthused with the vision of The Secret Society, but perhaps we could persuade you to think otherwise."

"Yes indeed! After all, you were allowed to return from the depths of hell to help us attain our goals, Miss Charlotte."

Lucretia lunged forward, pointing her finger at him. "Don't ever call me by that name again, or I swear, I'll cause you to die a long, excruciating death."

Holdsclaw chuckled. "You are an evil little witch, aren't you?"

"Continue to try my patience, and you will find out just how wicked I can be." She paused with emphasis. "Tell me about this grand plan that you and the Secret Society have conjured up, and how it's supposed to include, and benefit me."

"The plan is already in motion Ms. Darknight. We just need to secure your help in bringing Branch Consolidated into the fold."

"I quite understand that, but I'm not quite clear on what the Society's main objective is in all this."

"We want to increase the wealth among our members, and block any others from reaching our class level."

"In other words, creating a two-class society."

Holdsclaw and Lapino exchanged smirking expressions. "Exactly! For years, we've strategically placed our people in government, the media, and into positions of the business world. We're poised, and getting very close to seizing the United States for our purpose."

Lucretia rolled her eyes sarcastically. "What do you plan to do when you take control of the greatest country in the world?"

"We join with all of our foreign allies to form a one-world empire," Holdsclaw stated.

Lapino shook her head, laughing maniacally. "We'll be the kings and queens of the world."

Holdsclaw looked at her sternly, and she cowered in her seat, while Lucretia glared at both with disbelief. "You're absolutely insane. What will happen to those who are not part of the Secret Society?"

Holdsclaw stared across the table with an arrogant grin. "My dear Charl- Ms. Darknight! In every great society, there must be masters and slaves. On the political end, we make the poor and desperate think that we are on their side so we can get their votes. Then once we accomplish that, they're at our mercy."

Lapino added, "We'll simply drain all of their resources so that we can add to our wealth, and give them table scraps in return."

Lucretia shook her head in disgust. "And you have the nerve to call me evil?"

Holdsclaw cast an intimidating stare from across the desk. "Now, you listen to me. I happen to know your main intention is to destroy the Branch family and to take over Branch Consolidated. What would you say if I told you we could help make that happen?"

Suddenly Lucretia heard an interesting proposal that could suit her needs. "I'm listening."

"Other than the major investors, the Society has not been able to influence the insiders of Branch Consolidated. As we had hoped, you have been able to work your way into upper management. With that in our favor, we hope you might be able to swing some of the others over to our camp so that we can take over the company."

"What if I can't accomplish that? Daniel Branch has a very faithful following."

"Daniel Branch and Gerard LeRoux are staunch, old fashioned capitalist fools," Lapino said. "We're quite aware that they'll fight against us tooth and nail."

Holdsclaw eyed Lucretia lustfully. "But we're quite confident that a young lady with assets such as yours can somehow entice most of the others to join us."

"Then what?" she smirked.

"Then, my dear Ms. Darknight, we shall banish Daniel Branch, and his faithful followers from their own company, drain away their assets, and leave their families destitute. Much in the same fashion as his grandfather did to the Lockes."

"You still have Steven Spencer to deal with. He may prove to be quite a challenge."

Holdsclaw arrogantly said, "Oh yes! The bastard son who dabbles in the supernatural. I'll take care of him."

"I imagine the Society would assume total control over the estate of Branchview as well as Branch Consolidated. What would I have to gain for that?"

Holdsclaw answers with a clever smile, "We'll appoint you as CEO of the newly renamed Locke Enterprises, and I'll personally make sure that the Branchview Estate is turned over to you. That I promise."

Lapino jumped in, "So! Do we have a deal?"

Lucretia thought hard about it for a long moment. "How can I trust you to keep your promises?"

"You can't." He grinned. "After all, we are politicians. If you don't want to be a part of this, I will find someone else."

She paused for a moment and studied his face. "Then I suppose you can count me in. But I will warn both of you. Do not double-cross me, or you will deeply regret it."

Holdsclaw held his fixed smile. "I can assure you that our word is as good as gold."

Holdsclaw and Lapino rose and offered a handshake to Lucretia that she somewhat reluctantly accepted. "We do hope you'll attend next month's meeting at the SOS Club," Lapino added.

Lucretia answered with a slight smirk. As they left, Holsclaw turned to ask a question, "I'm curious, Ms. Darknight. What exactly are your plans for the Branchview Estate?"

She answered with venom, "I plan to burn the main house to the ground along with all the deplorable spirits that inhabit it. Then I'll build a new mansion on the ashes of the old Locke Estate that Daniel Branch the first destroyed."

Holsclaw pointed at her. "I like the way you think."

Lapino flashed an all-knowing smile. "Have a marvelous evening, Ms. Darknight."

She nodded. "I most certainly will."

Lucretia watched the senator and his colleague leave, then turned with a contented smile. The night had gone much better than she expected. It was the first time since she arrived that her plans were coming together.

The news of the upcoming nuptials brightened the mood at Branchview. As the family slowly made their way home from the funeral, they met in the sitting room to share stories. While they were reminiscing, someone knocked on the door, and Loraine turned to Steven.

"I'll get it." Loraine rushed to the door. Amy urgently stepped in with a very concerned expression. "Lori! Is everything alright? I got here as soon as I could."

"Oh, Amy! The past few days have been very arduous. I shall tell you all about it, but first I'd like to share some good news."

Amy tilted her head with interest, while Dr. Grayson entered from the sitting room and quietly observed. "Steven and I are getting married tonight, and I would like very much for you to be my maid of honor."

Amy reacted with mixed expressions of surprise, shock, and hurt, but just as quickly, she recovered. "Oh, Lori! I am so happy for the two of you, and yes, I would be honored to accept your offer." She embraced her with a very strong hug.

"Fabulous! Let me prepare you a glass of water, and we'll gather in the sitting room." Loraine exited, and Amy noticed Dr. Grayson, who offered an all-knowing look. "Hello, Dr. Grayson. How good to see you again?"

"You're in love with him, aren't you?"

"I beg your pardon. In love with who?"

"You're in love with Steven, aren't you?"

Amy chuckled. "That's ridiculous, not to mention quite impossible."

"Is it now? You might be the goddess of the sea, but you're still a woman. And honey, I can read your emotions from a mile away."

Before Amy could respond, Loraine returned with a glass of water. "We'll be sure to keep you adequately hydrated, dear."

Dr. Grayson whispered as they followed Loraine into the sitting room. "That'll be our little secret."

As the clock chimed at 9 pm in the foyer, Lucretia wandered up to the outside entrance, only to recoil at the sight of the wooden cross that stood sentry there.

"Does that cross bother you, my dear?"

Lucretia was startled by the man's voice; she turned to see the spirit of Daniel Branch the first, a handsome man in his early forties dressed in a Victorian-style suit. One feature caught her attention, his meticulously manicured handlebar mustache. She noticed his striking resemblance to Daniel III.

She blurted out, "It's you!"

"I beg your pardon, ma'am. I don't believe we've met."

Venom emerged. "Oh yes! I know very well who you are."

"If you know who I am, then perhaps you can tell me who banished me from my residence, and why?"

"I can only guess that it's because you're probably just as evil in spirit as you were in life."

Daniel was infuriated. "I… My dear lady! Who are you to make such an accusation?"

Lucretia waved her hand, and the likeness of Charlotte Locke appeared next to her. Daniel reacted with great shock. "No! It can't be possible…"

Charlotte announced, "Oh yes it can! I've come back in another form to avenge the pillaging of my family fortune and the killing of my grandmother and her children. I know you're responsible for all of it."

Daniel shouted back, "I may be guilty of many things, but I assure you that I had nothing to do with that dreadful fire."

"You're a liar! I know you hated my grandfather."

"True! Your grandfather was a Satanist and a philandering idiot. If anyone was responsible for that fire, it was more than likely him."

"How dare you!" Charlotte lunged toward his apparition, but he dissolved into the night air. "You're a coward, Daniel Branch! I command you to show yourself again! I know you can hear me!" Lucretia was left suspended for a time until Charlotte regained her composure, and once again merged with her likeness.

Inside the grand corridor, the room was lit up in old-world splendor as the family celebrated the wake, and prepared for the wedding at midnight. Steven played gentle music on the piano, and Mrs. Porter approached from behind, placing her hand on his upper back. "I wish your adoptive parents were here to see you. They'd be so proud."

Steven looked up at her as he continued to play. "I believe they are here, Mrs. Porter. Maybe the whole family on both sides." She smiled warmly and walked away.

Steven noticed one person in the room taking the situation especially hard. Daniel Jr was seated by himself, watching the proceedings. Since he seemed to be left out, Steven quit playing and moved over next to his side. "Penny for your thoughts?" Daniel answered with a sigh, and Steven smiled. "If you don't talk about it with someone, it's going to stay inside you, and continue to make you unhappy."

Daniel answered reluctantly, "I just don't understand why all these terrible things keep happening. I miss my mother so much, and now Marcus is dead. He was just like a big brother to me."

Steven leaned in closer to the boy. "When I first came here, I promised you that we'd do everything we could to make things better. We've had quite a few setbacks, but I still believe we can make that happen. Will you believe that too?"

He responded hesitantly, "I'll try…"

"Good… man, I knew I could count on you. If we work together as a team for what's good, there's not a power in the world that can prevent miracles from happening."

Daniel smiled at him. "I'm glad you're here, Uncle Steve."

"I'm glad I'm here too." Steven paused in thought. "I need you to do me a favor, Daniel." He sat up straight, "I'm getting ready to marry the love of my life, and I haven't asked any of the other men if they would be my best man. Would you play that role tonight?"

Daniel reacted with excitement. "You want me to be your best man?"

"Absolutely! Will you do that for me?" Daniel gave an enthusiastic nod.

The large clock in the corridor struck midnight, and Dr. Grayson sauntered over and tugged on Steven's arm. "Come on, Steven! It's time to do this."

Steven turned and winked. "Let's go, best man."

Dr. Grayson escorted Steven to the elevated stage at the head of the room. Steven then placed Daniel Jr. at his side and waited for the ceremony to commence. The room got very quiet for several minutes until the music began to echo throughout the room. Steven began to feel very nervous, then Daniel Sr. strolled into the grand corridor with the love of his life holding his arm. He suddenly got weak in the knees and found it difficult to stand. Daniel Jr. grabbed his arm. "I'm here, Uncle Steven. We're in this together, remember?"

Steven smiled. "Yes, we are."

Dr. Grayson waved to calm the room. "Dear friends! Earlier tonight we mourned the loss of our beloved Marcus, who I believe is still with us in spirit. But we all believe he would want us to remain strong as a family. He could never want us to linger in sorrow over his death, which is why we decided to see these two people married tonight. Well, this morning; on a very blessed day of the year, the birth of our Savior. We now…"

Amy moved to regain control of her emotions as she stood behind Lori. However, she was too late, as tears escaped and trickled down her cheeks, while Dr. Grayson continued. "If there's anyone in this gathering who objects to this union, let them speak now, or forever hold their peace." Dr. Grayson peeked over the top of her readers at Amy, who slightly shook her head no. "Very well! Best man, could we have the rings please?"

Daniel Jr handed Steven one ring, and he placed it on Loraine's finger. Tears rolled down her cheeks as Daniel handed her the other ring, and she awkwardly placed it on Steven's finger. Dr. Grayson then nodded at them, "By the power vested in me by the state of Connecticut, I now introduce you as Mr. and Mrs. Steven Spencer… You may kiss your bride, Steven." He looked up and smiled.

The room erupted as they kissed, however, the cheers are from more than the living individuals in the room. A thunderous accolade filled the room with blinding luminous light; everyone turned to look for the incoming visitors. Then within the glowing light emerged several apparitions, three figures to be precise. In the lead was Maggie Branch, while the other two apparitions remained in the light. She stopped in the center of the room and innocently proclaimed, "We're all here!"

The room was dead silent in anticipation as Loraine whispered to Steven, "This is absolutely amazing!"

Steven recited as though in a trance, "At the given hour, the chosen spirits of those who were dead will rise, and they shall be led by a child."

"Amen!" Dr. Grayson proclaimed.

Behind Maggie, another glowing light materialized, and the room waited with bated breath. No one could believe the sight: The spirit of Marcus approached his parents, and they greeted him with unadulterated emotion. But he quickly turned to Heather, who stood trembling with amazement. "You're here." She reached out to touch him.

"Yes… I'm here." Heather suddenly collapsed; Marcus grabbed her as she fell to the floor. It took her a few moments to regain some composure. "I'll be here in spirit for as long as all of you need me."

"I guess that will be forever then? Because I can't see me ever not needing you," Heather said. He smiled.

Since the room was preoccupied with the ongoing happenings, the third apparition moved forward. Penelope stood pensive, waiting for a view of the spirit. As the apparition materialized, an emotionally overwhelmed Amy glanced over at Steven.

He blurted out, "Oh, Dear God! It's my father." He smiled, but his interest remained with someone else. Penelope stood emotionally weakened. Jack gently placed his hand on the side of her face and stared admirably into her eyes. "Time has aged you just as beautifully as I always imagined it would."

"Oh, Jack!" she sobbed, "I missed you so much." She collapsed into his loving embrace.

Daniel Sr and Jr watched with amazement. "Uncle Steve was right. Miracles do happen." Daniel Sr attempted to disguise his emotion but failed. He smiled at the emotional outpouring. "This will truly be a night that we shall never soon forget." The room vibrated with positive energy as a chorus of voices echoed in unison across the high ceiling.

Amy turned to Steven and Loraine who were now conversing with Mrs. Porter. "It sounds just like a thousand angels singing."

"It's the most beautiful thing I've ever experienced," Mrs. Porter announced.

As the family greeted long lost loved ones, the turmoil was building outside of the grand corridor.

Charlotte looked on through the windowpane in astonishment. "I don't believe this! How can it be possible?" She turned away with desperate anger. "They will not win. I will stop this atrocity." In frustration, she waved her hand and vanished into the cold night air.

Inside the grand room of Branchview, the apparitions of past residents had now taken human form to be seen joyfully mingling, dressed in the unique attire of their given era. Like some magical dream, the miracle of the night continued. Along the walkway, outside the main window, a black cat strolled past, curiously looking inside for a long moment. Its sad eyes were almost pleading to be a part of the mystical festivities. It lingered a few moments more before it aimlessly wandered off into the dark cover of the night.

Chapter Twenty-Three:

Dawn's Light

In the cold twinkling light of dawn, Steven was still brimming in the afterglow of the previous night's events. It was a wonderful moment in time, celebrating the night away amongst present family, and the countless spirits of ancestors from bygone eras. As the household slept after reveling until the early morning hours, Steven offered to escort Amy back to her underwater kingdom.

"Amy… My head is still swimming after last night. In my wildest dreams, no one could ever imagine such an event could take place, especially on Christmas Eve."

Amy gripped his arm ever tighter and smiled as they strolled along the pathway. "It was a storybook moment. One that I shall never forget."

"I'm so glad you were able to share it with us."

"I wouldn't have missed it for the world." They both exchanged smiles.

"As soon as you're able, I need you to come back, so we can work on a strategy to fight the witch."

"I wholeheartedly agree. I'm certain the witch is already plotting her next move as we speak."

Their conversation was halted when a man in his early 30s with a muscular build stepped onto the path. His locks of luxurious dark curly hair laid against his shoulders. "Well! My dear, where have you been? I've been looking for you."

Amy reacted sheepishly. "Philip! What on earth are you doing here?"

"I should be asking you the same thing. You were missing, so I came looking for you."

His eyes darted suspiciously between Amy and Steven. "It's not what you think… this is Steven Spencer. I served as the matron of honor at his wedding last night, and the party didn't conclude until the early morning hours."

Philip focused on Steven. "Let me offer you my deepest congratulations, sir. My name is Philip Seagraves. I'm Amy's husband." Steven's eyes widened with surprise,

Amy reacted uneasily. "You might know him by his real name, Poseidon."

Steven chuckled. "You can't be serious."

Philip answered with a clever smirk. "I most certainly am."

"You do believe I'm Amphitrite, don't you?" Amy asked.

"I'm sorry if I doubt you, but it just seems so surreal. Me having a conversation with a god and a goddess. It's not a common occurrence with us humans."

"I would've thought that after last night, you would believe that anything was possible."

"Well, I have studied the supernatural quite extensively. But, the idea of mythical gods is all new to me."

Philip flashed a confident smile toward Steven. "I can escort my wife the rest of the way. I'm sure you're quite eager to get back to your newlywed wife, Mr. Spencer."

"Of course! I was just being a gentleman. It was a pleasure meeting you, Philip. I wish you both a Merry Christmas."

Amy smiled. "And the same to you, Steven. I will return in a few days."

Steven stood in complete shock as he watched them walk away. The previous night was enough surprise, but now he had just met the immortal god Poseidon. As Amy walked away, she looked over her shoulder for one final glance. It was an expression of longing that made Steven's heart skip a beat.

Philip looked to Amphitrite with a clever smile. "You love him just as you did his father and his great uncle."

"Is it that obvious?"

Philip chuckled. "Painfully! I'm surprised his wife hasn't picked up on it."

"She thinks I'm a lesbian."

Phillip laughed heartily. "Why on earth would she think that?"

"Because I told her so that she wouldn't be jealous of me."

Philip mused, "Who wouldn't be jealous of you, Amphitrite? You are the most beautiful of all the Nereids. Need I remind you that I sought you out in all corners of the world to take you as my wife?"

"I suppose you'll never let me forget that tragic event."

Philip snapped back angrily, "I made you an immortal goddess. What more could I have done to please you?"

Amy halted to answer, "You could have given me the one thing that I wanted most, and that was love."

"But Amphitrite, I do love you!"

Amy shook her head in disbelief. "Then why have you had countless affairs, and impregnated nearly every Nereid that catches your glance?"

Philip answered boldly as they proceeded, "Because I'm a god, and I have needs."

"And I suppose I don't!"

Philip reacted with frustration. "I've given you the freedom to do as you choose. Countless mermen could make adequate suitors. Why do you insist on falling in love with every human that resembles Matthew Branch?"

"That's not a fair question to ask. I would've given up my immortality to be with Matthew. But your pompous pride couldn't handle that reality, so you killed him."

They both halted, and Philip placed his hands firmly on her shoulders. "Amphitrite! That's not true! I did not kill Matthew Branch. How can I ever convince you of that?"

Amy defiantly pulled away from his grip and turned away. "By helping me identify who the real killer was, and work with us to defeat the witch."

Philip fired back in frustration, "Why is that so important to you? Can't you see that none of your efforts will ever bring Matthew back again?"

Amy turned and faced him once again. "Maybe it can't. But I do know that if the witch destroys the Branch family, it may also destroy any chance of a future incarnation of his soul. I know that at some point in time, he will return to me."

Philip sighed. "You would wait that long for him to return?"

"I would wait an eternity."

Philip looked out over the Atlantic. "Then what would become of you and me?"

"If you had any compassion in your soul, I would hope that you'd release me so that I could find true happiness."

He gripped her shoulders more delicately. "Despite my status, I realize that I'm not perfect, Amphitrite. But I do have compassion, and I will do everything I can to help you defeat this witch."

"Thank you, Poseidon… your words mean a lot to me."

They exchanged warm smiles. "It's almost sunrise. We should move on."

Steven contemplated his experience as he strolled back to the main house. He couldn't shake the haunting image of that final glance he shared with Amy in the pre-dawn light.

The house remained still after the previous night's reveling. Dr. Grayson got up early, shortly after Steven, and sipped a hot cup of cocoa in the sitting room. The large fireplace made that room a popular spot on cold winter mornings. Besides, the amicable essence of the past night still lingered in the room. She was holding a music box on her lap, and listened to its now familiar song.

The sound of the front door opening echoed throughout the quiet old house, and Steven noticed Dr. Grayson sitting on the love seat as he passed through the foyer. She quickly closed the music box and pleasantly greeted him. "Steven! I would've thought you'd still be sleeping soundly after such a marvelous night."

"I offered to escort Amy back to the shoreline." She responded with a raised eyebrow. "The most remarkable thing happened on the way there. A man met us halfway, and introduced himself as her husband."

"Her husband?" she replied.

Steven nodded, "He introduced himself as Philip Seagraves, but..." he paused. "If we would've remembered our Greek mythology, Amphitrite was married to Poseidon."

Dr. Seagraves was flabbergasted. "Yes! And being that he is an immortal god, he also has the capability of walking on land. Amazing!" She paced the room, lost in her thoughts. "You're quite fond of Amy, aren't you?"

"Not the way you might think, but yes. After all, I just got married to the only woman I love." Dr. Grayson responded with a smile, and Steven moved closer to her. "However, I do feel that she and I have some sort of soul connection. It's as though I knew her in another lifetime."

"She is immortal. You may have been acquainted sometime in a distant past." They both pondered the possibility for a moment. "I'm curious! What did Poseidon look like? Was he the same likeness as the artists' depictions?"

Steven paused in thought. "To be honest, I thought he resembled a heavy metal rock musician more than he did a Greek god."

"Oh! But I'd bet that he was very handsome."

"Could you ever actually picture a woman like Amphitrite being with an ugly man?" They both laughed. "Since everyone else is sleeping, and I'm wide awake, I think I'll grab a thermos of coffee, and take a stroll through downtown Lockeport. Would you care to join me?" Steven asked.

"I would like that very much; the fresh air would be very nice."

"Good… I'll be right back. Grab your coat, it's a bit nippy."

Steven headed for the kitchen to grab the coffee, while Dr. Grayson grabbed her heavy coat, gloves, and a hat.

Lucretia was wide awake at the cottage as well. She wandered into the kitchen wearing a long red lace nightgown, slit clear to the base of her hips. She leaned against the counter, grabbing a coffee mug to pour a hot cup.

A sudden chill swept through the room, and Lucretia turned to see Marcus boldly standing there, yielding a shiny steel sword in his right hand. "You!" she screeched. "What are you doing in my house? You're supposed to be dead."

"My soul will never rest until I get redemption for the life that was stolen from me."

"I had nothing to do with your death, Marcus. I avenged it by killing Tyronde, and saving your sister. Now I command you to leave this place, and go back to your grave."

Marcus laughed. "You have no control over me, witch. I'm a spirit of light, and the worst enemy that those of your kind could ever have."

Lucretia trembled with anxiety. "I'm not scared of you."

"You should be." He casually looked down and picked up a book that was lying on the kitchen table. "The Works of Aleister Crowley. How befitting for such a dark soul as yourself." He sets the book back down. "I know who you are, Lucretia Darknight."

"What do you plan to do about it, ghost?"

An evil glimmer covered his face, and his intense emotion caught Lucretia off guard. Marcus grabbed his sword and impaled the book. She moved backward as Marcus snatched the book off the table and held it in the air. "Lucretia, I was granted this sword by the angels. Every person whose soul has perished at the hands of evil possesses one, and it is powerful enough to fight any dark force on earth." The room suddenly became completely silent as he slammed the book off the tip of his sword onto the hardwood table. "This is the sword that will one day destroy you, Charlotte. But until that day comes, I will haunt you constantly, and protect the ones I love from your dark magic."

Lucretia growled, "We'll see about that—"

"Yes, we will! We most certainly will!"

Marcus faded from sight as his laughter echoed throughout the cottage. Lucretia's eyes desperately darted to all corners, looking for any other lurking spirits. The whole ordeal left a lingering feeling of malevolence in the room.

On the streets of downtown Lockeport, winter gusts blew in from the Atlantic, as Steven and Dr. Grayson strolled along the sidewalk. It caused Dr. Grayson to grab the collar of her coat with a shiver. Steven looked over. "Are you okay?" She nodded.

"Yes. That wind off the ocean is dreadfully cold today."

"It certainly is. I hate to think about it, but we probably have at least four or five more months to endure of this weather."

She nodded. "I want you to know that I plan on staying around for as long as it takes to get this problem resolved. However, I do need to start working on my book."

"I understand. Lori and I also have contracts to fulfill, so we need to start on our projects as well. Unfortunately, some of these spirits seem to have a different agenda."

"What should we do about Lori? We can't have her being fully involved during her pregnancy."

Steven came to a halt. "You're right! Once Charlotte learns that she's pregnant, I'm afraid she'll try to do everything she can to harm Lori and the baby."

Dr. Grayson's eyes lit up with a thought. "What?" Steven blurted out.

"I've got it! Lori could oversee the spirits at Branchview, and we could take care of everything else."

"Good idea! The more she can learn from those spirits about the family history, the better we can understand the agenda that Charlotte is trying to carry out."

They continued walking, and Steven took notice of a large building across the street that had Greek-style architecture, with large columns in the front, no windows, and a sign carved in the stone of the marquee that read SOS Club. "SOS? That must be a fraternity of sailors. Perhaps it means Sons of the Sea."

Suzie McVea approached them on the sidewalk. "Mr. Spencer, Dr. Grayson! Merry Christmas!"

"The same to you, Suzie."

She also looked across the street to the SOS Club. "That place gives me the creeps. I noticed you two looking at it."

"What can you tell us about it?"

"Not much! I do know that the Locke family built it around the turn of the 20th century, and there's a lot of urban legends about what goes on in there."

"It looks vacant. Does it ever get used?"

"About once a month, the parking lot is filled with quite a few high-end vehicles with out of state license plates, and some of the people come into the diner. They're quite an odd bunch, and they're very secretive about what they do."

"Do you know anyone from around here that's been inside the building?"

She shook her head. "No one that I know. If it wasn't for that one weekend of activity each month, I'd swear it was vacant." Steven and Dr. Grayson exchanged a quick, suspicious glance. "Oh well! It was good seeing you both. Tell Heather I'll stop by Branchview later today."

"We'll certainly do that, Ms. McVea."

They continued their walk, as Dr. Grayson mumbled to herself, *SOS...SOS...Where have I heard that before?* She came to an abrupt halt. "Steven! I think I know what that place might be." Steven waited as she concentrated. "I recall hearing my colleagues talk about an ancient secret society that is thought to be prevalent among some of the country's wealthiest individuals. It's also rumored to have several secret chapters among students at the Ivy League universities."

"I think I remember hearing whisperings about that same thing. What's the name of this secret society?"

Dr. Grayson answered with a foreboding expression, "Within their gathering, they refer to themselves as the Servants of Satan." Steven responded with a wide-eyed expression as he turned to look at the building once again.

Chapter Twenty-Four:

Overseeing His Ocean Kingdom

The morning sun climbed higher in the sky, somewhat warming the brisk air current blowing along the coastline. Steven and Dr. Grayson strolled on down the sidewalk, continuing their survey of the town. It was turning out to be an enlightening day in their quest to solve the issues at Branchview.

Below the cliffs at Lighthouse Point, Poseidon sat calmly overseeing his oceanic kingdom. One of his favorite spots was the rocky outcrop near the lighthouse, not far from where Amphitrite often sat to meditate. As the waves clapped against the rocks, a man with dark features, appearing to be in his late-thirties, with piercingly intense eyes and dressed in all black, approached from up the beach.

Poseidon watched with little enthusiasm as he strolled closer. "Little brother! It's been a very long time since we last talked."

"Not long enough by my standards, Hades."

Hades chuckled, puzzled as to his brother's true intentions for calling on him. He then climbed up on the rocks next to him. "I hope you didn't summon me here to exchange insults, on Christmas Day no less?"

"Actually, I brought you here hoping you might provide information about a particular murder that took place here in Lockeport."

Hades flashed an evil grin. "And what favor are you willing to do for me in exchange for that information?"

Poseidon looked at him intensely. "Absolutely nothing! Have you forgotten that I am also a God, and that I'm just as clever and cunning as you?"

"Fine! When did this murder take place, and who was the unfortunate victim?"

"His name is Matthew Branch, and he was murdered at the turn of the 20th century."

Hades laughed. "Do you think I have a filing system that keeps track of every murder from the beginning of time? I don't involve myself in such petty human behavior. I simply handle the consequences that follow."

Poseidon stood up. "I should have known that this would be a waste of time. Even if you knew, you'd have no intention of telling me."

"Wait! I can offer you this much." Hades stood as well. "You already know that many members of the Locke family were faithful servants of Satan throughout the centuries and that many feuds existed with the Branch family during that time."

"Yes! I'm aware…"

Hades took a deep breath and continued, "There was one member of the Branch family that was so evil in his own right, that even the demons envied him. His name was Daniel Branch. He lied, cheated, and even killed his family members to advance himself in the world. Perhaps this is the man responsible for the death of this Matthew Branch."

"And perhaps it could've been one of the Lockes that was responsible. My estranged wife, Amphitrite, has blamed me for this murder for over 120 years, and I'm determined to clear myself as a suspect."

"Ah yes! The beautiful Amphitrite. Please, give her my regards." Hades flashed an evil glare that failed to intimidate Poseidon. "Now! There's one simple thing that I'd like to ask of you, Poseidon." He listened reluctantly as Hades stepped closer. "We've always made it a practice not to involve ourselves in each other's affairs. Isn't that so?"

"What are you getting at?"

Hades grinned. "My associates are plotting a takeover of the United States. When they achieve this task, they plan to establish a one-world system governed by a chosen servant of Satan. Since I provided you the name of a worthy suspect, I would like to ask that you do not interfere with their plans, and in return, I will promise to not disturb any part of your precious kingdom." He extended his hand to Poseidon. "Do we have a deal?"

Poseidon responded with a hardened glare. "No way in hell! I will fight with all my powers to prevent that from happening."

Hades responded with a sneer. "Very well then, Poseidon! The next time we meet will be in battle. A prelude to the war that will end all wars."

Poseidon answered with boiling anger. "So it shall be."

The interaction between the gods has steamed up the area, and Poseidon and Hades matched each other with an enraged stare. Neither one was willing to give an inch; hence the war between the powers of good and evil had begun. It was a Christmas Day that would not soon be forgotten.

The members of the Branch family had begun to stir after their night of pleasant revelry. Loraine strolled into the Grand Corridor in a dreamy state. All the years she spent with Steven had finally paid off; she was now the wife of the man she adored. As she wandered through the room, she was unaware that Maggie was watching from the shadows. She stopped in front of the painting of Daniel Branch I, and spoke aloud to herself. *The negative vibrations just permeate from that picture.*

Maggie emerged from the shadows unnoticed. "My brother wasn't a very nice person."

Loraine looked down at the little girl with surprise. "Maggie! How long have you been standing there?"

"I've been with you since you walked in. I didn't want to disturb your thoughts." Loraine smiled, and Maggie soberly pointed back at the wall. "My other brothers' pictures should be up there too."

Loraine glanced at the wall, then back to Maggie. "Brothers? I met Andrew last night. Is there another one?"

Maggie soberly nodded. "His name is Matthew. He couldn't be there last night."

"Why not? He would've been openly welcomed."

"He was there, but his soul and spirit live in someone else. Someone very close to us."

Loraine was perplexed. "Where are these pictures of your brothers?"

"Daniel put their paintings in the storage room of the East Wing shortly after they both died."

Loraine paused in thought. "Isn't the East Wing an unused portion of the house?" Maggie answered with a nod. "I must get the key from Mrs. Branch. I would like very much to see those pictures."

"No! It's not safe," she blurted out. "No one has been in that portion of the house for a very long time." Maggie moved closer, gently placed her hand on Loraine's abdomen, and looked up at her with innocent blue eyes. "There's babies in there." Loraine seemed surprised. "Yes, there is! But only one baby that I know about."

"There's two. A boy and a girl," Maggie proclaimed in a matter-of-fact tone.

Loraine looked at her with astonishment. "How do you know for sure?"

"I could feel their energies when I touched you."

Penelope entered the room, and Maggie faded back into the shadows.

"Lori! Or should I say, Mrs. Steven Spencer?" Loraine responded with a pleasant smile. "Did I just see Maggie in here?"

"Yes, you did. She was telling me about the missing pictures of her brothers that are stored in the East Wing. Would you happen to have a key for that portion of the house?"

Penelope answered with much anxiety. "I'm afraid I don't. My late husband was the only one who had a key, and he forbade anyone else from entering that portion of the house."

"Would you have a clue as to where he may have kept the key?"

She shook her head no. "I've searched everywhere for it. Unfortunately, that's a secret that he took with him to his grave and beyond." Loraine looked perplexed. Somehow, they needed to find that key.

Steven and Dr. Grayson walked most of the morning, arriving back at the house before lunch. The rest of the day was more or less a coming down period after the high point that everyone had experienced the prior night. Most everyone kept to themselves in their portions of the house.

Loraine went to bed earlier than Steven that night. He stayed downstairs and visited with his mother and Daniel, then finished his evening playing the piano in the Grand Corridor. By the time he came upstairs, Lori was sound asleep. At the foot of the bed, Bumpers rested, alert to any potential occurrences that might take place.

After a few short minutes, Steven also drifted into a peaceful dreamscape. Suddenly, he found himself in 1897 Lockeport. It was the Camden Hotel lobby, in the late evening hours. The elaborately designed room was bustling with well-dressed people in Victorian-era garb.

A small table sat on the edge of the commotion, yet amid all the happenings. The woman seated there looked oddly familiar. Her name was Amanda Green, and she was dressed in elegant clothing suited to the time. Her bright green dress was the perfect contrast for her fiery red hair and spectacular blue eyes. In the chair next to her was Matthew Branch. As the dream vision cleared, the woman's identity became crystal clear. Amanda Green was another alias of Amphitrite. Her long red locks lay delicately against her shoulders with her veil covering part of one eye. Matthew's resemblance to Steven was uncanny.

He reached across the table and took Amanda's hand. Their eyes locked in an intense dreamy stare. The action in the room suddenly disappeared when their emotions took over the scene. "Amanda! You must try to convince Poseidon to release you. I want you to marry me as soon as possible."

"I promise you that I will talk with him tonight. I so look forward to the day that I can finally be your mortal wife, and never have to go back to the water again."

Matthew lowered his voice, "Are you certain that you want to give up your immortal role to spend but one lifetime with me?"

"Oh, Matthew! I've never been surer of anything in my entire existence. You're the only man that I've ever truly loved." He gently kissed Amanda's hand, while onlookers smiled and nodded approvingly. In the center of the room, suspended from the ceiling, an enormous ornate clock chimed at 11 pm. Amanda was saddened by the sound. It meant that she had to leave her beloved Matthew and return to the water, and the husband that she didn't love. "I must go," she said regretfully. He replied with an equally saddened nod.

Matthew stood up to pull her chair out as they departed, and made their way through the bustle of people. On the pathway to Lighthouse Point, they strolled hand in hand under the moonlight, and stars of a balmy mid-summer night. "What an extraordinarily beautiful night. It's one that I shall never forget," Amanda proclaimed.

Matthew gazed at her with loving admiration, "You are the most beautiful woman I've ever seen. It's amazing how your skin glows under the light of the full moon. It almost makes me wish that summer nights like this could last forever."

Amanda took a deep breath and sniffed at the air. "It's been nearly a week, and the smell of smoke from the fire at the Locke Estate is still in the air. I so wish I could have done something to prevent that tragedy."

"I know. Unlike my brother Daniel, I never wished any harm on the Locke family. Especially the children."

"You're a good man, Matthew Branch."

Their walk was coming to an end as they reached the overlook above Lighthouse Point. The ocean was calm, serene, and the moonbeams sparkled on the water's surface. Matthew cradled Amanda's face in his hands as they passionately kissed. "I'll meet you here again at sunset tomorrow evening."

"I'll be here." Their hands remained clasped until they were an arm's length apart before they reluctantly let go.

Matthew watched Amanda disappear into the darkness before starting back on the path to Branchview. He walked along with a dazed, fixed smile on his face until he heard a rustle among the brush. "Is there someone there?" He waited a few moments but the noise seemed to pause. A few seconds later, a rush of fear shot up Matthew's spine as something approached him from behind. He tried to whirl around to face the aggressor, but it was too late. A hardened rope had already been slipped around his neck. As he struggled in vain to free himself, the tension cut off his oxygen. In a few short minutes, Matthew's body fell limp to the ground.

Suddenly, Steven was thrust from his slumber, after experiencing the horrific murder of Matthew Branch. He woke gasping for air, grabbing at his throat. Loraine was startled by his nightmare and sat up next to him. He was frantic over the incident he had just witnessed in his dream. "Steven! What on earth is wrong?" He remained quiet. "Please Steven… talk to me!" She glanced around the room in desperation as Bumpers observed with great concern. "Help! Please! Someone, help us!" Steven fell limp onto his pillow as Loraine embraced him. "No! No!" she sobbed.

On the rocks, near the beach at Lighthouse Point, a silhouette of a mermaid goddess could be seen sobbing uncontrollably. She gazed out into the dark abyss, still heartbroken after all these years over the loss of the only man she ever loved. "Oh, Matthew! When will you ever return to me?"

Upcoming Branchview Saga

Branchview – The Epic Showdown

In this episode of Branchview 'The Epic Showdown' while, Steven is transported to another time, witnessing the murder of Mathew Branch, a larger plot by the Secret Society is growing to overthrow the U.S. Government to eventually establish a World Rule.

This sets the wheels in motion for an inevitable showdown on the expansive grounds at Branchview. One in which the forces of good and evil supernaturally clash on the heels of a massive Hurricane brewing offshore in the Atlantic.

Branchview – The Portal of Time

Stay Tuned with all updates on Branchview.info

Follow Me:

Facebook: @ infobranchview

Instagram @ infobranchview

YouTube @ Brian Jay Nelson- Screenwriter

Website: branchview.info